DAMAGED BILLIONAIRE BOSS'S BABY

AN AGE-GAP, ENEMIES-TO-LOVERS, SURPRISE PREGNANCY ROMANCE

ARIA McDOW

ARIA McDOW PUBLISHING

CONTENTS

1

CHAPTER ONE

J ade

Nine in the morning, I hear his voice barking orders as he comes closer to his office. I sit, back-straight, at the desk outside his office in my mini pencil skirt, plunging cotton shirt, and short leather boots. Red, of course. Nothing like a splash of color for confidence. Breathe girl, just breathe.

Suddenly I don't know what to do with my hands. Come on, get your shit together. He's just a man. Yeah, a super grumpy asshole of a man I could never stand to be around.

No biggie. I'm just the new personal assistant he knows nothing about.

Go work for Brock, Dad says. It'll pay well. You can finally get your own place and have a proper career. Proper career! My parents will never take my Sexologist qualifications seriously.

Judging by my first three clients, neither will the rest of the world. Sucks. Just because I'm twenty-two they think I'm either a pay-for-sex service or I can't possibly have the experience needed to advise them on sexuality. I'm far from being a virgin, though admittedly it has been a while.

Living at home, with a father who believes I'm the eternal virgin, and four older brothers keeping track of my social habits around DC, is a major cockblock combination. And let's not even get started on Mom repeatedly reminding me I'm cockblocking her and Dad! Sheesh. I can't even...

Brock Anderson's voice is still booming. Getting closer. Just keep thinking of the one-fifty-a- year salary with medical. Dad's right, I do need money to get my own place and I'm not too proud to accept this offer, though I may be stupid to accept it. Okay, most definitely stupid.

He barely even glances at me as he strides past. "Great, another pain in my ass behind a desk. Suppose you'll be off crying by the end of the day like the first four this month."

He smashes past me and touches his fob to the electronic keypad to open his office door. "Doubt you can make a decent coffee, but I'm dry enough to choke anything down at this point."

Son of a... thinks he's so above the human race he doesn't even acknowledge people with eye contact. My blood boils. I won't be treated like dirt under his feet or anyone else's. I stand, straighten down my skirt. Pick up the stack of printouts I've been working on and strut my stuff straight up to him.

"You're right. I make shit coffee. Luckily, I'm not here to make you coffee but if you're such an aficionado, grab one for me while you're there." I slam the stack onto his chest. "These all need your signature. Oh, by the way. Hi Brock, nice to see you again. Not. Me? I'm just great. Thanks for asking."

His large, well-manicured hand holds the folder to his chest. Dark eyes bore into me. "Jade?" His thick eyebrows jerk upwards. Eyes wide but ever focused on mine.

Energy zaps through my entire body. Keep it real. "Cream and sugar, thanks." Fake smile.

"How the hell did you get here?" His brow furrows and crinkles form at the corners of his eyes.

"Usual way. Mom and Dad had sex, clearly." My neck hair prickles, he's so close to me. Waves of bad energy pulse off him. Shit. I know every eye in the place is on us right now.

"You always had a smart mouth." Dead-pan face.

"Always will." I'm not scared of him and I'm no pushover. "I give as good as I get." His stare pins mine, and I fight the urge to step back.

"I bet you do." His harsh appraisal travels the length of my body, lingering a beat on my plunging neckline on the way back up to my eyeline.

My nipples tighten. Damn, why did I choose the sheerest shirt I own? My heart pounds. He's way broader than I remember and taller up close. I don't break eye contact. He takes a step back. Ha! I win.

He looks around and I know everyone else just pretended to not be transfixed on our encounter. "My office. Now."

"You can at least say please. No wonder you can't keep assistants. Just rude."

"I have no clue why you're even here. If you don't like how I do things, best leave now." His voice is lowered, but no less dangerous.

"I'm here because my Dad likes you for some unknown reason and he asked me to come bail your ass out. You can thank me later."

His chiseled face now looks like thunder. "Can we *please* continue this in my office?"

Oh, that low growl thrums to my core. This man is a born serial killer, I swear. I'm not sure I'm safe behind that door with him. "Seeing as you said please... okay then."

I follow him in, and he slams the door shut behind me. "Why don't I know I'm now a babysitting service for your father?" He practically stomps over to his desk to drop the document stack. *Whatever.*

"You're the one throwing a tantrum."

"It pisses me off when I'm not informed." He rakes his fingers through the mop of black waves on top of his head. "I don't have time for this shit." His desk phone rings. He snatches it up. "What?" His eyes latch onto mine once more as he listens and nods. He doesn't look any happier.

"I appreciate you helping out, but a heads up would have been better, Gary," Brock shifts the weight on his feet. His tailored black suit looks impeccable.

It's my Dad calling. I try not to smile.

"I see. Well, I guess in that case... Yes, yes, of course. Talk later." The phone hits the cradle. "I freakin' told you. Now, I'm a childcare facility."

"I'm not a child." I could just whack him one...

"Oh, I suppose eighteen makes you feel like an adult." His mouth lifts up on one side and one eyebrow tilts... I'm not even sure that classifies as a smirk. More a leer.

"I was eighteen when you tried to tell me what to do four years ago. Didn't get you anywhere then. Won't now."

"Eighteen! Surely you were sixteen."

I'm not sure at this point if he's trying to get under my skin on purpose. All I know is, it's working. "That was when you snitched to my parents about me playing hooky."

He grunts. Does he find that amusing?

"I don't need looking after."

"Really? Why does your father want me to take care of you then? Protect you from all the bad men…" His sarcasm drips thick and slow like honey.

I walk back towards the door. He won't get the last word. "Dad never said that. He wants me to help you get organized. Then maybe you can get over your Daddy issues and finally run this company."

Oh boy, that touched a nerve. He's in my face in no time. "I don't need your help and I don't need someone else's kid weighing me down." His brow furrows so deeply when he's livid, and his pupils are lost in the darkness of his brown eyes. His intensity pummels my bravado.

I take a step back and I'm hard up against the closed door. Fuck. Brock steps forward again like there's no such thing as personal space. Excitement I shouldn't be feeling flashes through me.

"You can leave anytime." He raises his hand between us to point at me and brushes my already rock-hard nipple. Did he do that on purpose? So help me, I squeeze my thighs together because if this was anyone else, I'd have him flat on his back on the desk right now while I showed him I'm no kid. Nothing like angry sex.

Not to be beaten, I poke him in the chest, his muscles have no give at all. "I'm not going anywhere. I'll have you for wrongful termination if you try and fire me."

He grabs my hand in his searing grip and pins my arm to the wall. "You have no clue how powerful I am, *child*."

I swear I can feel his swelling brush my hip. Fucking child, I'll give him fucking child… my other hand snakes up into the back of his hair and I fist it tightly, pulling his full lips towards mine as I whisper, "I'm *not* a fucking child!"

I kiss him hard, inviting his tongue to dance with mine. I nip his lips and take my fill of his expert mouth. I'm wet in my panties now. My heart is hammering and oh yeah I want his cock hard inside me. I may have been in control of this kiss at the start, but now his mouth owned mine and I let it happen. Opening to him, letting him take what he wanted. Let him get out of control. That is a win for me.

I press my hip to his erection and rub ever so slightly. He groans into my mouth and pulls me in tighter against him. Everything throbs in desire for him.

Suddenly, he rips out of the kiss, and I release his hair. "Get out of my office. Now!" His throaty growl is filled with emotion, "before I fail the only adult person left in this world who gives a shit about me. The job's still yours if you want it. Just keep it professional. Stay away from me otherwise."

Well, that was unexpected. Maybe the man does have a heart. I'm trying to gather myself to look normal for my re-entry into the world outside his office door. I realize I've crossed a massive boundary to prove a point. That was so stupid. He's my father's best friend.

Deep breath and speak in a calm, professional tone. "Suits me. I'll make coffee. You sign those documents. They need to be mailed. Please."

I am worried about what Dad would think, but I'm more worried that this man who embodies the corporate fat cats I despise has almost given me an orgasm from a single kiss. Imagine what his mouth could do in other places. It's a tough gig to find someone I don't like, but I want to have sex with. Always end up friend-zoning them and I won't risk sex ruining the friendship.

But finding someone I'm attracted to, but I definitely won't friend zone, may have just fallen into my lap. My skirt is straight, and I smooth my hair as I march back out to my desk, not acknowledging the interest from other employees, I head for the kitchen to make coffee.

When my college sweetheart, Charlie, comes back, maybe we'll fall back into an easy relationship. Maybe he'll be ready to settle down and start the life we spoke about while lying under the stars. His current backpacking trip is just a phase he's going through. Of course, he didn't have to go through it with a busty, eighteen-year-old natural blond...that hurt.

But we'd agreed... or rather Charlie talked, and I nodded... that seeing other people would solidify our commitment to each other in the end. I'm free to enjoy my body however I please. Love isn't an option. Charlie ticks all the boxes on my soulmate list. All except for one. He isn't here. But I do need to research my profession if I'm ever going to be taken seriously.

A little fun can't hurt.

2

— · —

CHAPTER TWO

B^{rock}

I pull at my collar and tie...What the actual frick just happened? Unbelievable! There can be no other girl...*woman* in the world who is more off-limits to me than Jade fucking Madison.

Her father has been my only friend and mentor since he started at this company thirty years ago when I was just fifteen. I cannot disappoint him. He trusts me with his youngest child. *His only daughter.* I pace to my desk. She's twenty-three years my junior. With any luck she'll suck at this job and I can let her go by the end of the week.

I sit and go through the stack Jade shoved into my chest. It's every single thing that needs signing from the last month. None of the last four assistants even took note of catching up on what I was behind on. What time did she start work, five in the morning? I work through, checking them over and signing each one.

Finally, this week is looking up and I'm making progress. Desk phone sounds. I look at the caller ID. My father. Scratch that, the day just went back to the shit-pile.

"George." was never allowed to call him father or Dad. "What's up?" He never called unless he had a criticism to detail out to me or some impossible 'head of marketing' tasks.

"Brock. The Delaney contract is up for grabs. You land it, you'll be CEO."

Yeah right. Another one of his reminders about how I'll never be true CEO material like him. "What about Lex?" My cousin, who is so far up George's ass, you can only see the soles of his shoes.

"He's got nothing to do with this."

"I find that hard to believe."

"Delaney wants you at his resort to discuss the details next week. Take Gary Madison's daughter with you."

"Wait, you know about my new PA?" Clearly, I am the last to know.

"I'm the one who okayed it and worked out her employment contract."

Of course, he is. Gary went to him to get her access. Makes sense.

Jade and I on a tropical island resort? Dangerous as hell. Her curvy body in a bikini is not anything I need in my face right now. "I'm not sure she's available... and I have Kieran at home."

"Not negotiable. She has to go, or you don't get the shot. Kieran has a nanny, doesn't he?"

"You know he doesn't. He's my son, I take care of him." Because I'm nothing like you.

"Take him with you."

"He has school. I can't just take him out for the week."

"Work it out. I had to with you. Not like I had your mother at home after she ran off..."

My knuckles go white around the phone. Every chance he has, he reminds me of the fact my mother left. Like it's my fault. Maybe it was, maybe she couldn't handle a baby. Maybe she couldn't handle what a tyrant my father is. Why didn't she take me with her? "Not like I have Susan at home either since she passed from cancer."

Not that George had even bothered to attend her funeral service. Bastard probably didn't even recall my four-year marriage.

"It's now or never, Brock. If you want to be CEO of my company, even though I'm not holding my breath you want it badly enough, get Delaney's signature. Do everything in your power to secure it. You need to toughen up."

"I'll work something out."

"Good. Well, we'll see, won't we. I won't hold my breath waiting."

The man is beyond belief. I should just ditch his ass and this company. But something inside keeps me trying for this CEO position. I could take it to the next level with my marketing skills. George never put much faith in my ideas. One day I'll prove it to him.

Shit, what can I do with Kieran? He's just seven and not used to being without me for too long. The only other people in this world I trust with him are Gary and Lisa, Jade's parents. Worth an ask since Gary got me into this situation.

I call him.

"Brock, how's it going?" Gary always sounded like he knew a joke no one else knew.

"Do you know the Delaney contract is up for grabs?"

"Ahhh, no. I don't." I can tell he's being straight up.

"George called. Says I need to take Jade to the Island Resort next week and seal the deal with Delaney for the new luxury build contract."

"Okay. I honestly didn't know that."

"Look, I'm not very happy about you blindsiding me on Jade being here, but I see George was involved so it's sure to be shady. If she can do the job, fine. But I need somewhere for Kieran to go and I don't trust many people, as you know." I trust only two people in this world. Gary and Lisa.

"Lisa will be stoked to have him stay and we'll see he gets to school on time."

"No candy after dinner, extra sugar gives him nightmares."

"Copy that. Don't let any of those lechers near Jade."

"Right." Fuck, now I'm a lecher! "I'll bring him around Sunday afternoon."

"Stay for dinner. It's been a while."

"Maybe when I get back." Juggling Kieran and George's schedules doesn't leave much time for socializing.

"I'll hold you to that."

A dinner that isn't just Kieran and I would be good for him. His mom always made sure we had family dinners around the table. I can't risk being there if Jade still lives there. What if she runs her mouth and Gary catches on?

The door opens and Jade sashays back in carrying a coffee mug. I push the documents back toward her. "I need a whole proposal by next week for Delaney. I'll email the details. Do some digging and see if you can find a point of difference I can come in on."

She nods and picks up the stack. Close to her voluptuous breasts I'd brushed my hand against. I wish it was my mouth. Shit, focus. Jade is off limits.

"Also, you're joining me next week at Island Resort to pitch. Orders from George."

Her already large eyes get larger and the sky-blue sparkle shows she's interested. "How long?"

"We leave Monday morning, be back by Friday, I hope. But not later than Sunday."

"Right. Do I get free time?"

"Normal business hours for you. Rest of the time you can please yourself. However, you are representing the company so please bear that in mind and tame your actions accordingly. Any little wiff of scandal can be something that loses this deal."

"Guess you don't think I'm a little girl anymore. Now I'm being accused of what? Gang bangs or public sex?"

I cannot afford for her to do or say anything to offend Delaney. This deal is mine to lose, and I did not intend to lose it.

"It's company policy, don't take it personally. I have no interest in what or who you do behind closed doors. Just don't do anything I need to cover up or lie about to your father."

"Bit late for that."

"Just check yourself." I really mean stay the hell away from me.

"I'll try to keep my rampant sex drive under control."

"Hopefully you do better than here today." I look at her mouth edges quirk up a little. Delectable full, ruby lips I want to devour again, but I know I can't.

"No desire to repeat it so don't get your hopes up. Just proving a point. Send the email."

I stiffen. I'd like to fill that smart mouth with my... Stop. No. Keep it professional. "Do your job. That's literally all I need from you." I watch her hourglass figure flow out the door. Damn.

This trip is important. This trip means I get the one thing I seem to have been striving for my whole life. Recognition from my father. To be good enough. I wasn't going to fail it and I'd be keeping my dick inside my pants. No matter how much it may want a showing. Not happening.

Fuck it. I won't let my friend's trust in me be destroyed. Gary wants Jade to be okay and not taken advantage of. I get that. From what he said, she's naïve but that kiss was as expert as any kiss I've ever had. I shouldn't have goaded her, but it's what I do best. I did not expect her to devour my mouth.

I send out the company details of Island Resorts and their last marketing campaigns by our biggest rival company. If I can land this contract, Anderson Construction will build the next five hundred luxury bungalows on the island along with a hotel fit for royalty. This is a billion-dollar job. While this company had made many billions in its fifty-year reign, this would be our largest single contract. Delaney's are the hardest contracts to land in Washington DC.

The marketing campaign to get forward bookings would also be up to us. That is Anderson Construction's point of difference. Not only can we build to a high spec, I make killer marketing campaigns to get sales rolling before the builds are even started.

My mind wanders to my son. This was the first time I'd ever left him this long since Susan passed three years ago. My heart pounds at the thought. Logically, I know he's safe with Gary and Lisa, but I also know he'll feel it a little. I know I'll feel it a lot. I can't let it distract me right now.

I pull up my file on everything I'd been saving on Delaney companies. There has to be something everyone else has missed. I have five days to work it out. I sip the coffee. Hey, this isn't bad! I gulp it down in a couple of swallows.

Even that doesn't get rid of the taste of Jade's lips. Strawberry vanilla or something similar. Her scent is much the same, soft skin, the type of booty any man dreams about and she knows how to work it.

I need to get her the fuck out of my mind. I better go see Gary and see how much budget we have in play for this offer. He'd been head of finances and legals since I first met him. That will kill the building libido I have for his daughter. Good healthy dose of guilt always got rid of any hope.

I walk out, straight past Jade. I don't speak. If anyone sees me showing her any positive attention around here, there'll be talk starting.

I stop off to give orders to the junior admin assistant. "I need every report I've emailed printed out in hard copy, sorted in chronological order and on my desk by the end of the day."

"Yes, Sir. Sir, are you aware that's over two hundred pages?"

"Of course I'm damned aware of it. I don't walk around with my head up my ass like half the staff around here. You better get started." I glare at the young man and he practically wilts.

"Yes, Sir, Mister Anderson."

"If you need help, call my PA, Miss Madison. No excuses. I don't have time for excuses, I only want results." Ah, that's better. Flex some boss muscle.

One kiss from forbidden fruit isn't enough to put me off my game. One thing is a positive. I don't have to worry about ever liking her. Jade Madison is not likeable at all.

3

CHAPTER THREE

Jade

Look at this massive resort! I've never been anywhere so opulent. Why can't Carrie be done with her final bar exam? I messaged her about how my life had turned around in a week. But no answer from my best friend. I mean, I get it, at twenty-one it's a big ask on your first try. But I really need my former college roommate now.

The single best thing about being here at Island Resorts is the fact I get to wear less clothes. This heat has sweat beading on my forehead already. I need a shower. I yawn. Wow. I can't remember ever being this tired. Getting this campaign together had me working late every night, except Friday.

I went dancing. Spent some of my hard-earned advance. Brock certainly returned to his true asshole state. I don't think he ever had a nice thing to say. But, I just signed a lease to a small apartment near Dupont Circle. Super-excited. And now, a tropical resort. For free!

I lug my bag to the counter beside Brock.

"They do have concierge, you know."

"I'm fine. Don't need to be waited on. I have arms and legs."

He rolls his eyes and tips the suited man pushing the luggage trolley.

"Mr. Anderson. You have the Honeymoon Penthouse. Our best." The mature woman behind the reception counter speaks.

"There's really no need to go to that trouble."

"Mr. Delaney insists. There's scotch and champagne waiting in your room and a selection of charcuterie to get you through till dinner. Do let me know if you need *anything* else."

Oh, I bet she'd be lining up to fulfill Brock's needs. Heads had been turning since we walked in. His presence commanded attention. After last week, they can damn well take him. He's such a drama llama.

Brock takes the card to open the door. "Thank you. I will."

The receptionist smiles. "I hope you both enjoy your stay."

"What about Miss Madison's room?" Brock's demanding tone rose in pitch a little.

You got that right, what about my room? I'm blinking at her, and she gives one of those close-lipped smiles like she knows we're trying to cover something up. Oh hell no. I'm not sharing a room with his shit attitude to life.

Not when I'm in paradise. Not when I can see so many hot bodies around and no parents or brothers raining on my parade.

"Mr. Delaney has only reserved one suite. The hotel is full. Most people are sharing. Haven't you heard the tropical depression forming may turn into Hurricane Arlene?"

"*Obviously.* I checked the weather. These things almost never happen this time of year." Brock doesn't attempt a smile.

"Perhaps, but travelers don't like taking the risk and airports shut down flights. So, they stay on and we accommodate them as much as possible."

"I'm happy to sleep in the broom closet." I ignore Brock's glare. Can't be professional having your PA prefer a janitor's closet over you.

I cannot be in the same room as him for a whole week. I will have to kill him.

"Mr. Delaney will be *very* insulted if you refuse." She looks at me like I'm the most boring thing she's encountered in her life.

Brocks dark eyes are drilling into me at this point. I've put in so many hours on this proposal. I can't go insulting Mr. Delaney now. Dammit! "I guess I can sleep in the walk-in closet or something."

Brock sighs and walks off. Oh, the Incredible Sulk. Good times. I guess I can always find someone who needs a temporary roommate. My time is my time. He said so. As long as I'm ready for work each morning and I'm not being scandalous in public, I can stay wherever the hell I want. I follow. I'll play along for now.

He's walking like a robot. No fluidity whatsoever in his body when he is angry. He's like a building with arms and legs.

I wonder how hard it is to get him to show some other emotions. I mean, he did when we kissed, but since then he's been like titanium. Not that I'm looking to be friendly with him. Nope. But if I can open him up a little, surely that proves my years at college aren't a waste of time. I need to believe that.

The palm trees bend in the wind outside. So much for a cocktail on the beach later. Guess I'll have to hit up the bar instead.

"I have everything we need to get started right away in my briefcase. I want to pitch as soon as I can," Brock says as we approach the elevator doors.

Raincheck on the bar as well. "Thought the evenings were mine? Only business hours, you said." We stop and wait for the elevator to open.

"Just a couple of hours tonight. I need to be on my game."

"I guess, seeing as you asked *so* nicely. Nightlife won't start till ten anyway."

Angry glare city again. "We'll have dinner in the suite. You need to be fresh for an early start."

"I may as well be home with my parents," I retort.

"You'll live."

I step in the elevator behind him, dragging my case. My text alert sounds. I'm barely out of the house and Dad is checking up on me, I bet.

Oh damn! It's Carrie! My stomach lurches as the elevator speeds to the top floor. I didn't expect this. I'm terrible for motion sickness, but in an elevator? The lift stops with a smooth lurch that turns my stomach again.

Another person steps in and pushes the button for a couple floors above and off we go again. I shove my cell back in my pocket and clutch my belly. Oh wow this is the worst. Don't vomit on your boss, girl. I give a groan.

"You get used to it." Brock lets me know once the elevator stops again and the other person gets out.

"I can make myself sick turning sharp corners when driving my car, so I doubt I'll ever get used to it."

"That beater wouldn't go fast enough to make anyone ill."

I snap my eyes to his. Was that a joke? Is he trying show a normal human emotion?

"You're an embarrassment to the company. Get a new vehicle," he demands with a scowl.

Of course, that would require him to *actually* be human, so, no. "Gertie has been through a lot with me."

"Naming an inanimate object. Why am I not surprised?"

The elevator is so quiet I only know it stops on the top floor when my stomach does a final lurch. "Well, your parents named you."

I swear the air turned to ice in that moment. The look on his face...he truly hates me. I don't move because I'm not even sure if I can with the waves of bad energy lashing against me. Okay. My bad. I don't seem to have a problem evoking dark energy from him. Should I apologize?

"I don't need you tonight. Stay away from me and don't fucking speak to me."

"I'm sorry. I shouldn't have said that. Obviously, you have deep-seated issues."

He storms from the elevator and to the door opposite, swiping the entry card. "Don't try and psychoanalyze me with a degree that you made up because you aren't smart enough to major in a real career."

Oh, screw it! I drag my case through the open suite door, pushing past him, not even caring about the contact. "I'll ignore that because I touched a nerve. But don't you ridicule something you can never understand. As if you can even give pleasure to a woman with your narcissistic nature. She'd have to fake it hard."

The slamming of the door echoes around the suite. He advances. I stand my ground. "Faking it when I kissed you, were you?"

"Firstly, I kissed you. Secondly, I've had better." Thirdly, that was a lie. My heart pounds, and the sweat on my brow is not because of the tropical climate, nor is the throbbing between my thighs.

"*Really.*"

"Yeah, really."

He pushes up closer still and my case crashes sideways as he fondles my hardened nipples through my sheer blouse. "These are faking it then?"

"Physical reaction, nothing more."

So, help me, my knees buckle a little as he pinches each one in turn.

"If I go down between your legs to taste this." He cups my mound and squeezes. "You'll be dry as a desert."

I can't speak. His eyes own mine and the heat searing through his gaze and his hand caressing me through my panties has my mouth open with a gasp. He claims me with his kiss. His masterful, experienced tongue takes mine to task.

Why haven't I considered an older, experienced man before now? It's like he knows my body already. I don't have to talk him through a thing. He breaks the kiss and dammit, I whimper. I fucking whimper. Who even does that?

That rasping, deep tone goes to my toes. "When I fuck you. And I will fuck you, Jade. You won't be faking anything." I went to say something but he ripped my blouse like paper, pushing my scanty bra from my oversized breasts.

Each chiseled nipple is sucked and nipped in turn as if he has all the time in the world. My panties are soaked now. He lifts me and carries me to the largest bed I've seen and lays me down, sliding my thin jeans and panties down at the same time. On his knees now and I can't stop him. I part my legs for him, knees bent.

He groans and presses his thumbs to me. Opening me wide for him. The pressure on my clit almost tips me over the edge. I grip the bed to gain some control. His hot, firm tongue gives a long swipe upwards. "Mmmmmmm," he moans.

I can't take much more of that.

His searing tongue goes deep inside me. Tasting everything I have and I fist his hair now, lifting my hips uncontrollably. "Don't stop," I beg.

But he does stop and I need him to finish this. I can't be left like this.

"Still faking it, Jade? You want me to make you come?" His gruff teasing is delicious. He stands and undresses, very deliberately in front of me.

Not to be beaten, because I know he wants this as much as I do. I circle my most sensitive place. "I can finish myself off if I need too."

4

— • —

CHAPTER FOUR

Brock

"Like fuck you will." I cannot stop. I know I should. Something about her won't let me. Like a challenge to please her because no one ever has. She's no virgin, but she'll feel like one after this. Seeing her playing with her clit, pleasuring herself has my cock rock hard and I push my briefs till they drop to the floor.

I stroke my engorged member, and she watches while licking her lips. But this massive erection isn't going into her mouth. Not this time. Jade pulls her knees back and I cannot stop the surging want and need I have for her right now.

"Fuck me, Brock. I need to come with you deep inside me."

I start slow. I want to plunge right to the hilt. But I edge my swollen head inside and she grips so hard I fear she'll force me back out. I nudge in harder, deeper and a condom crosses my mind. I need to get one from my wallet.

Jade cries out and reaches forward to grab my ass cheeks as she pulls me into her. Crying out as she does. Before I know it, she has flipped us and I'm on my back. How did that happen? I don't care as she let's her tightness impale onto my hard rod.

"Oh fuck. Brock. So good. So good."

I feel too close to the edge. I need to slow her down, but she holds me tight within her and rides me hard and deep. I tweak at her nipples and the ripples of her climaxing pussy begin to massage my cock. I can't take anymore. I can't stop her as she leans over me, gasping, screaming and shuddering through her whole body.

I flip her on her back, in command again as I drive up inside her and my come let's go. I always had control. Always. Not this time. I feel I'm being ripped inside out and nothing has ever felt so good. I cry out her name and her nails are in my back, heightening my pleasure. I look down and she looks right at me, watching me come, enjoying that I have no control. But neither does she as I continue to ride her through her shockwaves of her receding orgasm.

When I'm spent, I collapse over her. Geezus. What did I just do? My best friend's daughter. I promised. No fucking condom. I pull away.

"That was a mistake." I drag my briefs and suit pants back on.

"Why?" she asks.

"For one thing, I promised your father."

"Oh, buzzkill."

"Secondly. I had no condom and that's been building up for a while."

She grins like she's proud of that fact. "Same. But, I get a three-month injection. And I don't have any sexual diseases. I can show you a report."

"Now who's the buzzkill?"

"Wait...was that joke? I mean, are you being funny?"

I can't help but give her a half-grin. "I can be funny when I want."

"Let me mark this on my calendar." She's getting dressed now. "So, do you have a health screen?"

"I always, present company excepted, wear condoms. I will organize a screening if it makes you feel better." I'm trying to rein my control back in. "We have work to do."

"You said you didn't need me and to stay away from you. Besides, I'm hungry."

"Dinner, then we go over that proposal for the last time before I pitch it tomorrow. If that's okay with you."

"Careful, you almost said please." She takes her case into the walk-in closet. "I'll take the couch tonight."

"What?" Did she just say what I think she said?

"I'll sleep on the couch. Just because you proved I wasn't faking, and neither were you by the way, doesn't mean I'm shacked up with you. You still annoy the fuckery out of me."

"Feeling is mutual. And yeah, you can take the couch."

"Chivalry is clearly lost on you."

"Equal rights these days, you know."

"I will share the bathroom. But you stay out while I'm in here."

"Bit late to be shy when I've just had my tongue deep inside you." I need to stop this banter. Get back to being professional. I cannot let any feelings creep in. Feelings get you hurt, devastated. Destroyed inside.

"Maybe I'll return the favor later." She marches into the bathroom.

What the hell does that mean? Is she even serious? Do I really want to know?

***

"Anderson. You're on time. I like that." Delaney's voice boomed out across his office.

I'd been waiting here for thirty minutes. I want to say, pity I can't say the same about you, but I bite my tongue.

I stand and shake his hand in a firm grip. He's balding, gained some weight since I last saw him, and I'm pretty sure he's just turned eighty. But his mind is still sharp as a tack, and I know how he likes to use any Achille's heel he can find. I have to be very careful. That's why I came to this meeting on my own.

"Good to see you, sir. I hope we can come to a suitable agreement."

"Come sit at the desk. Didn't you bring Jade with you?"

Interesting. "I did. She's working on some last minutes things for the pitch."

"She has a bangin' body and I bet she can suck dick with a mouth like that."

Anger rises. "I beg your pardon?"

"Come on, Brock. Don't tell me you haven't fucked that smart mouth of hers."

I stand up now. Anger boils up inside. "I'm not here to talk smack about my assistant. Can we get to business?"

"Your father told me he had a firecracker to help seal this deal. Told me you'd bring her here for me. You did good, Brock. I just need a week and I'll sign. I'm bored with all the yes girls. I need some fight." His eyes shone with sick expectation.

Fight is exactly what he'll be getting if he keeps up with this. What had George done? Is he a fucking pimp now? That man is unbelievable. "I think we have our wires crossed. I'm here to pitch. Miss Madison is here to assist me. I can hardly order her to stay with you a week, can I?"

"I know you've had sex with her. Stop trying to pretend otherwise. Maybe her father would like the recording." His cold eyes stare at me.

I'm shocked. I can't even speak. Is he saying what I think he's saying? He had our room bugged?

"You leave her here next week and I'll destroy the evidence."

My disbelief morphs into anger and my fists ball up. "You are fucking sick. You won't blackmail me into making Jade do anything, just to get a deal done."

"She won't be. I'm simply asking for her company for the week and with me needing some expert advice on penile dysfunction, I'm sure she'll cure me with her Sexology degree. His sneer made me sick. "And I'll be so grateful I won't be able to hold back. I mean, it's barely any different than you taking advantage of her. I bet her father won't even care. He knows what a slut she is, that's why he got her a real job. I do my research."

I launch across the desk at him and drag him by the collar towards me. "Don't you fucking spew that disgusting talk about her or my friend," I growl.

"Some friend," he sputters. His sick grin taunted me. "You couldn't wait to fuck her."

So help me, I know I should let him go but I want to snap his neck like a twig. "There is no deal to be made here. I'll leave today." Thoroughly disgusted, I let his collar go and he rubs at his red throat.

"Good luck getting out of here with this weather. I already emailed her an invitation to stay on next week, in her professional capacity, of course. I guess it's up to her."

"Stay out of my way, Delaney. Keep away from Jade. I will tell her what a vile creature you are if I have to. But I don't want to sully her with your filthy ideas." I had to get off this island somehow. At least out of his resort. God only knows where he has cameras.

How do I tell Jade? Do I tell Jade? I slam the door behind me. And people think I'm an asshole. He is sick. I'm going to call George and tell him to shove his damn CEO position up his ass. When I think of what he may have done before in cahoots with men like Delaney, I shudder to my core. I don't need him or his business.

I take the elevator back to the suite, pacing the small space like a caged panther. "Pack your things, we're leaving here." I bite out the words as I enter the room.

"Meeting done already? wait... what?" Jade is looking at me with wide eyes and raised brows.

"I'm not staying here another second and neither are you, Jade. Pack your fucking bag." I roar knowing I can't tell her yet just why. But I will, as soon as we are out of here.

Jade is frowning now. "The weather...we can't fly out. They say if it makes landfall in the next few days, this island could be ripped apart. The locals, we have to try and help them."

"Fine. If we can't fly, we'll find another place to stay."

"But why? I don't understand."

I go to her and take her face in my hands. "Jade, please just trust me now. I need to get you out of here. We'll talk about it later."

I saw something in her eyes I hadn't seen in a very long time, from anyone, but especially a woman: acceptance of trust she didn't even know why she had to have. But her blue eyes soften, and something between us shifts. She does trust me.

While I've broken her father's trust, at least her being with me is better than whatever other darkness lurks in this resort. I have to keep her safe. And if that means in my arms, that's the way it has to be until we can get off this island.

5

CHAPTER FIVE

Jade

What's got Brock this upset? He's more than angry, he's desperate. Desperate to leave this resort. I don't understand. What the hell happened with Delaney?

We're at the front reception again. Different receptionist there now. Can't say I'm unhappy about that.

"There must be somewhere we can go," Brock insists.

"Sorry, Mr. Anderson. Everything is full. The hurricane is coming and communications have just gone down."

"What? Fuck." Brock pulls his cell out and looks at the screen. I do the same. The woman is right. No signal.

"No landline either, sorry," the receptionist adds.

"Are there taxis running out there?" He points outside with a jerk of his hand.

The receptionist shrugs. "Hard to say. Most won't be but some locals who need the money might run the risk."

"I'm going to check. Don't you move from here," Brock commands as he pulls me away from the counter and lowers his voice.

"Hang on a second. I'm not a pet. Tell me what's going on." How hard can a free week at a luxury resort fuck up? Only on day two. New record of life fails right here.

"I will. I promise. Let's hope a local driver may have somewhere we can go. Somewhere not owned by Delaney. *Please*, wait right here for me?"

Damn, why can't the female goddess inside me say no to this man? "Don't be too long." He's making me nervous now.

He gives a half smile and squeezes my hand. I check my phone again. Still no service. Lucky I got a message to Mom and Carrie when I did. This impeding hurricane is all over the news, and I had let them know we were safe and sound. Might have peaked a bit early there. I was safe and sound until Brock decided he has to drag me outside without a clue where we can go.

It's like jumping out of a perfectly functioning plane. Why would you?

I watch the doors like a hawk. Brock almost gets blown back through them. "I have a car and a driver. It's rugged out there."

"Shit. Okay. I'm ready." I grab my case handle and Brock gets his in his grip.

His other hand covers mine tightly. "Hang on out here. The wind is gale force. The car is directly across from the door."

I nod and as we exit the resort, I'm thankful for the strength of Brock. The gale rushes through the pick-up area and I stumble a little before getting my bearings. I see a white car and we head towards it. A native islander gets out and opens the trunk. His massive hand takes my case and swings it into the opening and Brock puts his in. The driver opens the back seat door and I scramble in. Brock meets me from the other side. The doors close and for a second I enjoy the shelter of the vehicle. The driver gets back in.

"You know a place we can go?" Brock asks him.

"Other...hotel?" he asks.

"Anything that isn't owned by Delaney." Brock's face has hardened. What the hell happened at that meeting?

"Hah! Good joke. You no like Delaney?" He asks in slightly broken English.

"I need to keep her safe." Brock points to me.

The driver looks at me and nods like he knows some secret. Then talks back to Brock. "I know. Only one. Retirement place."

"Do you mean an old folks home?" I'm not sure this is sounding very luxurious or romantic.

The driver questions me with his look in the rear vision mirror.

"You know, um elderly. Grandmas?" Not that I'm ageist but this stay has reached a new low.

He laughs and nods. "Ah, yes, yes. Some are grandmas. Some just rich."

"But it's not owned by Delaney?" Brock is like a dog with a bone on this.

"Kind of. His sister. He wants to buy her land. She say no. She no like him either."

"Will they have room?" Brock asks.

"She make room. Make room for everyone. Nice lady."

"Let's go."

He starts the car and turns to Brock. "I hope we make it. Trees down, water over road."

I see his frown and I'm not feeling confident.

Brock hands him a stack of hundred-dollar bills from his wallet. "Will this help?"

"Sure. Sure thing." The driver grins and takes the money, stashing it in his shirt pocket. "I try my best. Thank you, thank you. Help my family."

"Good," Brock replies.

"Ten kids. Eat lots."

"Ten! Wow, I struggle knowing what to feed one." Brock's voice is pitched high.

"Oh, one no good. Lonely. Needs company, lots brothers and sisters." He stares right at me in his mirror.

"Oh no...ummm, no. We're not...you know. We're not together like that. He's my boss." That sounded so lame. Am I blushing? No. No way am I blushing.

"Ah...yes. Sure." He winks at me and puts the car into gear.

Brock's hand is burning through my skin making me remember how he made me feel less than twenty-four hours ago. "What's going on with Delaney?" I ask him quietly, searching his face for any clue.

"I don't want to talk about it in the car." He reaches his arm around my shoulders, drawing me to his warm, muscled body. I melt into him. Even though this situation is temporary, it's nice to feel protected. Never thought I'd ever say that, but I guess I've never really met a man like Brock. His protection doesn't feel stifling. I won't go as far as to say I like him being around right now. But it beats him being grumpy.

***

"Wait, Brock, what are you saying?" I can't really believe what I'm hearing. I also can't believe we're in a tiny room resembling a slightly oversized closet with small, double beds.

"My father instigated you being here with me, getting this job, to cater to Delaney's crazed games. He wanted you here next week alone and he'd sign the contract over to our company."

"Does this stuff even happen for real?" Surely, it's just in the movies. Sex, blackmail, billion-dollar deals. "I mean, no one can make me do anything I don't want to do."

"Do you think I'd have us sleeping in this shoebox," he gestures about the room, almost hitting the wall with his hand, "if I didn't suspect the level his depravity may stoop to?"

"I can look after myself, you know."

Brock stared at me. "He had a camera on us in the suite."

What? Did my boss just tell me that we were filmed having sex on a camera that was hidden in our room? That did rattle me a bit as well as the implications. Brock is afraid to tell my Dad the truth and now he may have no choice.

Wait a minute. "But have you seen proof? Maybe he's bluffing."

"How would he know we'd been together otherwise?"

"I guess you've confirmed it with your reaction. Clearly, he was hoping for something to happen between us in that suite."

"True. I hope you're right. But even so, he does know now thanks to me not keeping my cool." Brock rubbed his stubbled chin. "I should've called his bluff and demanded proof."

"Are you worried he'll tell my father?"

"I am. I hate George even more for thinking this is okay. People are just business deals to him. He's always looking for the upper hand and he doesn't care who gets cut down."

I take his hand in mine. No one ever deserves that sadness in their eyes. What a shit life he must have had. "I'm sorry he's like that. I complain about my parents messing in my life, but I know it's because they care, at least."

"Your father always has your best interests at heart. You and your brothers." Brock looks into my eyes and my heart breaks for him.

"I can't imagine growing up with a parent that didn't know how to show love of any kind."

"George doesn't understand love. He's a freakin' monster. Zero care factor on anything apart from making money. He has no feelings for anyone. If it wasn't for your father...I'm not sure I'd even be here right now. I certainly wouldn't have been able to raise Kieran like I have..." he stops talking.

Though I'd love to ask, I respect his choice to keep his son private.

"Gary, you know, *your Dad*, trusts me with you. I promised to keep you safe. What do I do? Break his trust by having sex with you."

I take his hand in both of mine. "You *are* keeping me safe. You can't get safer than a retirement village." I smile. Trying to lighten the moment.

"Except I became the very person he wanted to keep you away from. Someone capable of taking advantage."

"Come on, Brock. Enough pity party. No one is taking advantage of me. I'm not an idiot." I lean up and kiss his lips. Both his arms come around me now, to hold me tight. My blood races around my veins.

"I guess you're not. Sorry for all the kid cracks. I really didn't remember you being twenty-two. The past four years have been such a blur." He rests his chin on top of my head. It feels so secure being held in his arms.

"Dad has to let me grow up. I choose who I have sex with, not him."

"I know he's ten years older than me, but your father is my best friend. There's no adult in this world more important to me. I don't want him thinking less of you, either."

"He can think what he likes of me." I shrug. "I'm not ashamed of being a sexually active woman. I love my body. I love the pleasure it brings me, and I want to show others how to reach a deeper understanding of each other and themselves through sexuality."

"You mean Sexology is really a thing?"

"Of course it is. This generation is in tune with their bodies. They know what they like and they aren't afraid to ask for it. Doesn't have to be about love, it can simply be about pleasure. Consenting adults, male, female or otherwise. There's nothing to be ashamed of."

"Knowing it and being that way are two different things."

"That's where I come in. We're here for the week. We're consenting adults. Neither of us are in danger of catching feelings. Why not find some pressure release through our bodies? It's healthy. Stress is the number one killer in modern society."

"I don't do love so that suits me. When you put it like that. I guess it can't be wrong."

A tap came to the door. "Afternoon tea is ready in the lounge. Come and meet the others." That's Gwen's voice. She'd welcomed us in, given us a hot toddy, and showed us to the room.

"We better go, I suppose." I hated to let Gwen down when she'd shown such kindness.

"I thought we were adults and could please ourselves?" He gave a full smile this time and the way his face changed blew me away. I see the playful side of him, and it warms my heart even more. Here is a man with real life scars and history, still doing the best he can for his son and trying not to let down his father.

That's a tenacity rarely seen in my age group. Most of the men I know around my age still live with their parents.

"We have scotch and if you have any loose change, bring it for the card table." Gwen calls through the door.

"This sounds like my kind of afternoon tea." Brock stood up and held his hand out to me.

"Sounds perfect." I let him help me up and he pulls me hard against him. The feeling of his hard body against mine has my heart racing. "Or we could…"

"Later. Let's go say thanks to our hosts and win some cards." Brock rubs his hands together and gives a lopsided grin.

"You're going to beat elderly folks out of their pension money?" I grin back.

"Sure gonna try." His lips lightly brush over mine. My need for him jumps at this gentleness. "Then I'm coming back here to win a few rounds with you."

"No feeling guilty afterwards." I can handle him not wanting love. I don't want love either. But regret is something I don't want to hear about. "Don't say how sorry you are that I've blown your mind. Doesn't do much for my self-esteem."

"Deal. No more pity parties. But I do prefer to keep this between us. Of course, it may still be on a recording."

"No one is hearing it from me. We'll cross that bridge if we come to it." I think an extra week here might be good to try and find out if there really is a recording of us. I bet I can get that information out of Delaney if he's that interested in me.

This messed-up luxury resort stay has taken an exciting turn. Sex on tap with Brock. No emotions involved. Can't get better than that. Bring it on.

6

—◆—

CHAPTER SIX

Brock

"Dammit. All I have left is my watch." I look around at the shining eyes surrounding the card table, watching Jerry and I play. "You lot have fleeced me. Thought I was getting old folk with bad hearing and even worse eyesight."

"I think you're the oldest one playing, Brock." Jerry laughed at his own joke. He was ten years my senior at least. We'd started hours ago with fifteen players. Now it was just the two of us.

"Very funny." I throw my gold Rolex into the middle. Winner takes all." I've not been this relaxed since...I don't even know. Maybe ever. Could be the fact there's no internet or phone service. Could be Gwen's hot toddies... "Gwen might have mentioned that the small change she referred to was fifty buck notes..."

"You should join us on our one grand minimum bet nights. They're fun," Jerry says with a laugh.

"I don't get it. Why are you all living here? You could afford a mansion each and no one is frail and in need of care here."

Jerry observes me for a few seconds before he decides to answer. "Lifestyle. We get to go under the radar and have a lot of fun. I've been here for five years. I like the company. It beats being lonely."

The cards are dealt, and I glance across to the sofa area. Jade is a vision with her wide smile and blue eyes. Blonde hair tumbled around her face. She attracted attention and I can tell she's not holding back. While many here are older, there are also plenty my age and younger. Men and women. Not as young as Jade, but that isn't bothering her.

I don't even have to care. Like she says, she is free to choose who she has sex with. Right now, I think I'm getting beat out by a busty redhead who wasn't at all shy about her attraction to Jade. Can't say the thought of Jade being touched by anyone else makes me happy.

"If you like it, maybe you shoulda put a ring on it." Jerry's voice wakes me from my daydream. "What?"

"You, staring at her like that. She your girlfriend?" Jerry asks personal stuff like he's known me all my life.

"She's my PA. My best friend's daughter." I glance back at her, her nose crinkles just slightly when she laughs.

"Oh man. You fucked." Jerry has a deep chuckle. "I know that look."

I snap my attention back to him. "I'm good. Can we just play cards?"

"As soon as you look at your hand. Been dealt for ten minutes. You gonna tell him you're dicking his daughter?"

"Geezus, Jerry. It's not like that." This man should work for special intelligence.

"What's it like? You in love with her? Gonna marry her?"

"No...can we drop the subject?" I pull at my collar and stare aimlessly at my cards.

"Sure," Jerry says with an air of feigned nonchalance. He pushes all his money into the middle. "Winner takes all."

"You're bluffing." I study my cards. Sweet fuck all in this hand, but that watch cost me twenty grand. I ain't parting with it. "I got this. Easy."

Jade glances across at the same time I do and we smile. I like how that feels. My wife and I always had those moments. I miss them.

"You been married?" Jerry asks.

He must be psychic. "You're trying to put me off."

"Getting a conversation out of you is like getting blood from a stone. Just trying to be friendly." Jerry grins at me.

I'm sure he's bluffing the cards. "I don't talk about my life."

He speaks as if he hasn't heard my last words. "I've been married five times. Divorced four, the last wife passed from cancer last year. Fucking devastating disease. No one can really understand that kind of loss unless they've lived it."

Does he have some kind of radar for topics I don't want to utter a single word about? "Sorry to hear that."

"Do you wanna get married? Have kids? I never had a kid. Think I regret that most in life." I hear genuine sadness in Jerry's voice.

"Being a father is the greatest." It slipped out while I was studying this shit hand like it meant something.

"There, you told me something personal and you didn't die." He laid his cards on the table.

His hand is worse than mine. At least I had a pair of tens. He had zilch. "Hah! Gotcha." I scrape all the notes and the watch back out of the middle.

"You win at cards. Suck at life. You better sort out this crap with your best friend or you're going to lose bigtime."

"Tell me something I don't already know." I exhale. He is right of course.

***

"Wow, I had the best time. I mean totally unexpected." Jade called from the small shower room.

"I know what you mean. Certainly not what I imagined a retirement home to be."

The bathroom door opened, and she walked out looking amazing in her silk nightie and robe. "Also, the rooms are soundproof." She winks at me.

"I'm not sure how you get to that topic in a conversation, but somehow, I'm not surprised in this place."

"We talked a lot about sexuality. All the ladies were very interested in my advice as a sexologist. It was nice for a change." She pads past me to the small double bed and sits.

"For a change?"

Jade sighs and her eyes are down. "No one takes me seriously, or they think I'm there to give live demonstrations with them. Ugh!"

"I see. What's your target market?"

"Anyone who has sex."

He laughs. Actually laughs. "Ahh, you need to niche that down, a lot. Consider this time here as market research. Now you have a room full of women, and probably men who take you seriously. Use that as your platform. Find out their needs and offer that as your service. Build out from there."

"At least they don't think I'm selling them sexual favors here. That's why I had to take this job with you. I need the money. Dad made me minor in business, so I have the skills, but putting the package together for my own enterprise is harder than I thought." I give a deep sigh. Finally admitting it to myself is hard. "On paper it looks good. In reality, I haven't helped anyone yet. Last thing I wanted was to work for a man I hate…"

"You hate me? Okay."

"I don't hate you, I guess. I hate corporate fat cats, living the high life while others are starving, working people to the bone for maximum profit. The two times I met you before this didn't exactly paint you in a positive light."

"That's a little judgy don't you think? Not all corporate moguls are like that."

***

Jade shrugs. "Maybe it's judgy, but I have principles."

"I can't disagree. When I look at the way my father runs his business. But when I have my own, I won't be anything like him." I absolutely believe that. "I'm going to shower. Keep talking. As for your business idea. It's really as simple as marketing it right. Let's look into it more when we're back home."

"Why don't you start your own business instead of wanting to run a company like that?" She has a valid question. The same one I've been asking myself for years.

I leave the bathroom door open a little. I guess it can't hurt to talk about some private stuff with Jade. Not like she was going to run back and tell anyone. "It's important to me to prove I can."

"I can actually relate to that. Sometimes I feel like my parents and brothers are correct about sexology not being a serious career, but I just can't help but keep trying to prove them wrong. So far, all I've done is prove them right."

"That sucks. I know. I've been at this way longer than you and it really never improves." I don't ever want Kieran to feel he has to prove anything to me. I want to prove I'm worthy of being his father.

"Thanks for the tip."

I know she's smiling out there. I'm undressed and in the shower. I turn up the heat and soap up my body. Oh, it feels divine after the day I've had. "You're welcome. Sorry I don't have better news." I turn and face the wall to let the water hit my back.

"I think I can make some good news."

Suddenly, I feel Jade's hands caressing my sudsy chest from behind. She's entered the shower and I'm hard in an instant with her lush body pressed to my back. I feel her nipples are hard and she plays with mine. I groan in pleasure. "Geezus that feels so good."

"You feel so good." Her hands trail down my abdomen.

I turn to her, my erection jutting between us. She encases my cock with both her hands and explores the length and girth of me. I throb as she strokes me.

"So hard for me. I like that, Brock."

"You make me hard, woman," I growl before I kiss her open mouth hard, fisting her hair in my hands. I thrust into her tight hands covered in soap as my tongue explores her sweet mouth.

She cups my balls and squeezes. Fuck yeah, that drives me crazy. I pull out of the kiss. "Careful, I might have to bend you over and lose myself inside you."

"Be my guest." She turns around, steps out of the shower and places her hands on the basin, staring at me in the mirror. "Let me watch you fucking me."

I need to be inside her so badly right now, but I'm not doing this without a condom. Not this time. "Hold that thought. I'll get the condom."

"No problem. Just hurry or I might finish without you."

Her hand is between her thighs now and she moans as she shuts her eyes, touching herself.

Damn, that's hot. I rush to get a condom from my wallet. It feels like forever to open and get on.

I hear her sounds of pleasure and stride back in, unashamedly hard and ready. She opens her eyes and watches me move behind her again. "If you want to watch me fucking you..." I move her to be more side-on to the basin, "This is a better view."

"Hurry." Her breathing is heavy and her fingers are still working on her clit. Her eyes are glued to my erection close to her.

I part her with both hands and slide inside her, long and deep and hold my full length inside her. Her tightness ripples around me and she pushes back against me. "Oh babe, you fill me so good."

I swear I'm going to lose control, and I've barely moved yet. I slide out almost to the tip and go in deep again. My hands grip her hips.

"Come on, give it to me hard. I need to feel your cock driving me hard." Her guttural tone tips me over the edge and watching the pure desire on her face makes my need become uncontrollable.

I begin to fuck her deep, hard, and fast. Just like she wants it. I really hope these walls are soundproof because Jade is crying out my name as she works her clit in perfect unison with my thrusts. When I can take no more holding back, her orgasm erupts around my cock and her pussy clutches me inside her as I come hard.

I yell her name and pull her back harder on me as I lose every last drop of me inside her. When I open my eyes, we make eye contact in the mirror.

"That was hot as Hades," she says with a breathless laugh. "Wow!"

I grin, not pulling out. Her tiny tremors still feel good. "One of these days, I'm going to make love to you slowly."

"Maybe you need some professional help for being premature." She giggles.

I slap her ass cheek as I slip out of her, she stands to face me. "I'm not the only one." I kiss her lips gently. "I guess we're a hopeless pair." I hold her against me.

"I guess we are."

Jade isn't the first woman I'd had sex with since Susan passed...but she is the first woman I'd really wanted to make love to, not just have sex. Pity I couldn't control myself long enough to do that. "Let's go to bed. If that's what you want. I don't think I can fit on that two-seater sofa though..."

"I want that more than anything right now. Tomorrow is another day. Tonight, we have each other."

Gotta admit, I wish tonight would never end.

7

— · —

CHAPTER SEVEN

Jade

I'm not sure which woke me first, the banging on the door or my cell phone ringing. I hear Brock groan, but he doesn't move from spooning me and I don't move either. My phone stops.

"Hey, the phone lines are back up. No power yet but they are working on it." Gwen is calling through the closed door. "Internet is patchy but there. Seems the wind is dying down. It's almost time for afternoon tea."

"Thanks, Gwen." Brock calls back. "We'll pop out soon."

"What! Did she say afternoon tea? How long have we slept?" I ask and try to wriggle free.

"It was daybreak when we went to sleep." Brock mumbles and tightens his grip on me. "Can't we just ignore the world a little longer?"

As if on cue, my phone rings. I look at caller ID. It's Dad. "I have to answer, it's Dad."

"Shit. Okay." Brock releases me and I feel cold. I pull my top on and sit on the side of the bed.

"Dad. I'm okay. Storm is starting to ease up."

"I want you home. Now." He sounded as livid as I've ever heard him sound.

"I beg your pardon?"

"I want you home and away from *him*."

Shit, maybe there is a video. I play it cool. "Away from who, Brock?"

"Yes, and Delaney."

"I'm fine. There's nothing to be concerned about." Here we go again with ordering me around.

"Where's Brock? Put him on the phone."

"He's eating breakfast...ah I mean late lunch. I'll get him to call you back." *Breakfast...* way to go, Jade. I turn to look at Brock. He's lost a little color in his face. So much for no regrets. This is stupid. I'm a grown-ass woman not a child. Maybe I need that as a tattoo, across my forehead.

"Delaney is bad news, Jade. At this point, I'm not sure I can trust Brock and I never thought I'd say that," Dad continues.

"I'm not sure what any of that has to do with me."

"I don't want you getting used. You know... advantage of. You're attractive and innocent..."

"*Dad*. I'm twenty-two. The fact that you won't let me grow up is not my problem. I'm not innocent. I have sex, Dad, with anyone I please. Stay in your lane. I'm very capable of taking care of myself." I hang up. I can't deal with this any longer. It's stupid.

"That didn't sound good." Brock is getting out of bed and pulling on his briefs.

"Dad wants you to call him. Something about Delaney. I dunno, maybe there is a video. I'm done with this attitude of his. He needs to chill." I check my emails on my smartphone and see one from Delaney Enterprises. I open it.

I wasn't going to stay after being with Brock last night but after that call, I think I need to, to show Dad I can look after myself.

"Damn, sounds serious. I knew I shouldn't have let myself get carried away," Brock says.

"No regrets remember?"

"I know what I said, but hurting Gary is the last thing I want to do." Brock is dressed and headed for the bathroom.

"Go lie to him then. I don't care, but if he asks me straight up, I'm not lying to him. I'm also going back to the resort for the week Delaney has offered me." There, take that.

"Like hell you are. He is bad news. Period. I won't let you go back there."

I hear the water running in the basin.

I'm annoyed now. "No one owns me. You and Dad both need to grow the fuck up. Not me. Let me know when you graduate emotional kindergarten."

"Jade, I'm telling you Delaney is a creep and I don't think he'd stop at anything to get his way with you. You can't go back there alone."

"So, stay with me if you're so worried," I say, but I know darn well he has his son to get back to, so I use that to my advantage.

"You know I can't do that." His hand bangs on the basin.

"You also can't stop me from staying."

"You work for me. I need you in the office."

"That's easy. I quit." Hell, I'd just signed a lease. I still had to pay rent every month.

"I guess you got a better offer with Delaney. Typical." He's standing in the bathroom doorway, furrowed brow and eyes darker than ever. "What you're doing proves how immature you really are."

"How you're acting proves how stagnant you really are. I don't know why I thought I could find some real emotion inside you. Maybe I do suck at being a Sexologist after all."

"Sorry your little guinea pig experiment didn't work out the way you wanted it to." He began shoving his things into his case. "I'm getting out of here. You go do you." He slams the door closed as he leaves.

"I will." I called after him. How did we always end up here, at each other's throats? Guess we are back to hating each other.

***

Brock was right. Delaney is next level. But I did find out there is no video though. Delaney was bluffing about that. I can handle myself, but that man just scares me. I stayed four days after Brock chartered a private flight home.

As angry as I am about my father and Brock trying to run my life, I get it. I moved back to Gwen's retirement village two days ago. Tomorrow I'll fly home and try and find a way to pay rent next month.

Message tone. It's Carrie. I'd told her everything.

How's it going?

I'm flying home tomorrow. I'm over the tropics.

Guess what?

??

Saw him today...

Brock?

No, silly. Charlie!

What!!!????

You didn't know?

That he's back in DC? Nope.

Oh shit, sorry. Thought you kept in contact.

I think he lost his phone and contacts or something.

Yeah, anyway. Get home. I need wine with you.

Done deal. Bye.

Charlie is back? Why wouldn't he have let me know? Okay, I've been here on an island during a hurricane, no way he could've known that. He must have finally come back to his senses and realized settling down and making a commitment is a good thing. He ticked every box. Okay, the passion one was running on low, but I always thought we could work on that.

Is he back to make a commitment to me? He just needed time to find himself. He could never truly be happy with anyone until he was happy with himself. I can't wait to hear about all his experiences.

I wander out to the sitting area. A group of ladies all smile and ask me to sit with them.

"We've been waiting for you." The one with the whitest hair says.

"Really? Why?" A few I remembered from when I was here with Brock. I'd told them I was a sexologist, and explained what that meant.

The youngest of them, Betty, I'd met already.

"I told them what you do. The sex thing," Betty practically titters.

"Okay." *Sex thing?* Wow.

"We want to learn." Betty says in a hushed tone, looking around the room.

"About sex?" Surely these experienced ladies knew a thing or two already.

"About...pleasure." Her face went red amongst the twitters. All of them leaned in and nodded.

"You mean, pleasuring yourself?" I lower my voice to match theirs. They nod again.

"And," Betty whispers now, "is there really a G spot?"

"What's a G Spot?" one asks.

"Maeve, it gives you an intense orgasm," Betty whispers.

"I've never had an orgasm," Maeve replies.

From the heads nodding and shaking and the twittering, I realize what I need to do. This is awful. I'm stunned at this revelation. "Okay. Calm down. How many of you have never had an orgasm?"

Several hands raise.

"Right. How many of you have been given an orgasm by another person?" Hands go down, other hands go up. So that was five out of around fifteen that knew how to achieve orgasm. These ladies needed help to know their own bodies and what did it for them.

"No judgment. How do you feel about some workshops. Privately held here. Would you be willing to pay for that?"

"What are your rates?" Betty asks.

"Five hundred per person per session, plus expenses. But…"

"Done!" Betty walks around high-fiving the others.

I was about to say I'd give a group discount. "Ladies, I'll get back to you. I'll send Gwen details. I can work in small groups, males and females, or couples. Or this whole group if you want. Let's get you all hooked up on the pleasure train."

Maybe I'd been looking in all the wrong places for my clients. Trying to sell ice to the Eskimos. Brock had mentioned target market research and I'd ignored his advice. Maybe I need to listen.

Not sure he'd want to even speak with me. But I probably need to apologize for my outbursts now that I know what Delaney is about. The past two days here had been awful.

Not like I missed Brock or anything. But his work kept me busy, and I was good at it. How bad could a side job be? It is kinda fun pushing his buttons. Maybe he still needs a PA.

I sip the cocktail Betty brought over. Lord it nearly blew my head off. Eww, my stomach is turning. I can't take another sip, let alone finish it. I go to the bathroom and splash water on my burning face. I hope I'm not coming down with anything.

8

—◦—

CHAPTER EIGHT

Brock

"You're making Lex CEO, for real?" I glare at George and as usual he shows no emotion.

"You lost the deal. You gave it up for a bit of younger tail. Maybe you are like your father after all," George smirks.

"*Father*?" I spit the word out. "You've never been a father to me. I've only ever been in your way."

"I knew you'd give up on the deal. Zero stamina. Like your mother." He rubs his left arm.

"Don't blame my mother. How the fuck could she stand a man, no, a *monster*, like you?"

"Wasn't just me she couldn't stand, was it?" All that ever came out of his mouth was poison.

"I'm done with this business. You and Lex can fester in it together. I never want to speak to you again. One gift my mother gave me was her gene pool. At least I have half a chance of not being you."

I walk out the foyer doors and the sun hits my face. Freedom. Never even bothered to pick up my stuff from my office. Just a reminder of my years here striving for nothing. Let Anderson Construction fail.

I've got plenty of investments and plenty of my own money. No more fighting for a company I don't even want. Fighting for a legacy I'd be embarrassed to carry on. Kieran is my main concern, and Jade was right about one thing, I do need to be more open with my feelings, for my son. He can't grow up wondering if I love him, or wondering why I don't love him. I'll tell him every day and I'll show up every day. For him.

This conversation with Gary still has to happen. I never did call him. I'm taking the afternoon to make some memories with my kid. We might even take a trip… He'd had so much fun with Gary and Lisa when I was at Delaney's, I know I need to enjoy life with him a little more. Maybe Disney World without a cell phone. Perfect idea. School could wait two weeks.

Reality could wait for two weeks. I called my travel agency.

***

Two Weeks Later

"How good is that ice-cream cone, buddy?" We sit on the deck of our Disney World accommodation.

Kieran looks up at me and grins, an ice cream ring around his mouth. Happiness bubbles from inside me and I laugh. Damn, these past weeks have been amazing. No cellphone, no getting disturbed. No questions. Nothing to prove except that I love my son as much as life itself.

I look up and shade my eyes from the bright sun. I swear I see what looks like Gary's silhouette. The silhouette comes closer until I see clearly who it is.

"Brock…here you are."

What the? I'm completely caught off-guard at the appearance of Gary. "How did you find me?"

"We share travel agents."

"Right. Why are you here?" He can't have come to bust my balls over Jade. My stomach suddenly lurches. Jade? Has something happened to her with Delaney? I should never have left her there...I've thought about her constantly. Every blond woman reminds me of her and yet is no comparison.

He stopped at the steps. "Might be better if it's just us."

"Kieran, you can have movie time early today."

"Yay! Thanks, Dad. Hey, Mr. Gary! You wanna watch with me?"

"Not today, Champ. But we'll catch up soon." Gary gives him a huge smile. I can see he genuinely loves my boy, and I feel guilty that I can't do him the decency to tell him how I feel about Jade. That I like her, a lot. As a person.

Kieran nods and runs inside.

"Is Jade okay?" I have to ask. "I'm sorry I left her there with De-laney..."

"Yeah, yeah. This isn't about her." He shuffles his feet.

"Okay then. You aren't here for the ice cream cone."

"Your father...George. He's had a heart attack." Gary's face is ashen as he delivers the news.

"What? Where is he?" A swirl of emotions wash over me.

"He's, ahh, he's gone. They tried to resuscitate him, but...he didn't recover."

"Fuck." How am I meant to feel?

"I have a private flight waiting for you. There's more."

"More?" Even in death that man had a sting waiting for me.

"He left Lex the entire company in his will, and he plans to sell it."

"Sell the business?"

"Yes."

Anger burned inside me. I know Lex was going to be CEO but that doesn't mean he gets to just sell the company. "Over my dead body."

"Not a good choice of phrase."

"I'll get packed."

The flight was calm and fast. Back in Washington DC, I leave Kieran with Gary and Lisa so I can go see my lawyer. I'd save my conversation with Lex until I had professional advice. I also need to go look through George's personal effects at his home. There may be documents I need.

"Brock, Come back for dinner with us? Save you trying to find food later. I'm making Kieran's favorite," Lisa asked.

"Yay! Fried chicken and mac and cheese!" Kieran cheered. "Please Dad, can we?"

"I'm sure he's busy," Gary says.

"I do have business to attend."

"Nonsense. I can't stand his broodiness around here anymore," She nods her head towards Gary. "So not attractive and mama needs some fun." Lisa winks at me. "Time to sort it out. You know, be adults..."

I just stare at her.

"We'll see you at six. Kieran will be expecting you, so don't be late." Lisa grabs Kieran's hand and leads him inside.

"Six it is." I guess it will be okay because Jade doesn't live here. So that is one bridge I don't have to cross yet.

I drive to George's penthouse first. Better that I have as much as I can get to take to the lawyer. I still have a fob to let me in although I haven't come here since Susan passed. I didn't want Kieran anywhere near George.

The door springs open when I touch the fob against the electronic pad. I'm almost surprised George hadn't changed my access number.

Nothing looks any different in here. I walk through to his office. His desk is pretty bare. Nothing in the drawers. I wonder about a safe. He'd have one but I have no clue where or how to get into it.

I know it won't be somewhere obvious. I walk through the penthouse and open his bedroom door. His familiar cologne hangs in the air in here. I feel a pang of something. Not sadness...how can I? I never loved him.

I go to his walk-in closet. Full of suits, designer clothes. Much of which I'd never seen him wear. Nothing that looks like a safe. The top shelf houses some cardboard storage boxes. Worth a look.

I pull down three. There's a year written on each one, probably shoes he never wore or something. I flip the lid off the one marked year 2000. I stare at what's inside. I have to look hard to even believe what I'm seeing. I rip the lids off the other boxes and they are the same, full of envelopes with my name and address.

What? I tear one open and unfold the letter with shaking hands. I can barely hold it still long enough to focus on the beautiful handwriting. I can't read it through the blur of unshed tears but I see *Dear Brock*...and flip to the last page...*loving you always, Mom*.

I see all these boxes on top of the shelves. So many. That bastard had never given me the letters from my mother. How the fuck could he do that to me? Why did he need to punish me so much? I ran out to his bedroom and smashed everything that was breakable.

How can I hate him enough? He's not even here to face me. I can't do this. I can't. My heart is breaking in ways I never knew it could. After I lost Susan, I didn't think anything could ever hurt as much. I was wrong. This does. This hurts me to my core.

I sink to me knees and the tears fall freely. I have no clue what to do. I know what I want to do. I want to say goodbye to this shitty world, full of hate. But I think of Kieran. I think of Gary. I think of Jade. I get off of the floor, I'm taking every last box with me and I'm never coming back here again.

Lex can sell the business, hell, he can sell this penthouse. I want to wipe my father from my life forever. I'll cancel the lawyer appointment. But what will I do with all these letters? Am I strong enough to read them all alone? If it was a multi-million-dollar business deal, no problem, but this was my heart and my heart is broken again.

I need to pull my shit together for Kieran and dinner. My trunk and back seat are full of these boxes, there must be thirty at least. Should I go by my place and drop them off. I'm not sure I even want them in my house. What are they going to say?

I keep driving back to Gary's. I just need to talk this out with the only person I trust right now. One thing I do know, I can't read these alone. But tonight, I need to talk about how much I detest the very ground George walked on. I need support.

9

CHAPTER NINE

Jade

So, Charlie *is* back. He's crashing on my sofa right now. His eighteen-year-old travel companion dumped him for a native villager in Samoa. He's broke and has no job prospects. He also loves me and wants to settle down.

Yeah, what a flipping turnaround. This is what I wanted. For him to go away, come back to his senses because he couldn't live without me, and come back to settle down. My soulmate, my one and only true love.

But Charlie is nothing like I remember from two years ago. He gave me a hug and went to kiss me and I couldn't stand it. I pushed him away. He needs a place to stay and I've given him a week. Which is now up, but he's still asleep over there and I have a client call at Gwen's Retirement Home to do.

"Charlie, wake up!"

He groans a little and moves slightly. "Babe, chill. Just another hour."

"I'm not your babe and you need to leave. I have a business to run. Get. Up. Now."

"Fine. Business? You don't mean...as a Sexologist?"

"Of course I do."

"Huh, I never thought that was really a thing that would work for you. I mean and a career in something you were so bad at..."

He said what now!? "You supported me through it all at college, saying what a solid choice it was. It's you that's bad at it. I had to give myself every orgasm."

"I didn't like to upset you. You know how your temper is." He says this like it's a normal conversation. How did I ever be with him for four years?

That's it. Time to stop the bull shit. "Get out of my apartment."

"See what I mean? Brutal."

"I have to go out to the deli. You have an hour to get out of here."

"You know I'll give you another chance. We were good together."

"I'd rather stick red hot pokers into my eye sockets."

"Fine. Suit yourself. Do you have any cash? I need bus fare."

"Fucking walk, you moron." I slam the door hard and race down the two flights of stairs as the elevator is broken, again. How dare he? He wasn't a man. He didn't even compare to Brock's big toe. What a hide Charlie has to say those things to me.

Bad at sex! I wish Brock was here to tell him how great I am at sex with a real man, not some man-child looking for a free ride and bullshitting his way through life.

My cell rings. So help me, if this is Charlie... It's Mom. Okay, phew.

I connect the call as I walk down the sidewalk. "Mom, hi. What's up?"

"I'm making fried chicken and mac and cheese for dinner. Haven't seen much of you since you got back."

"I'm sorry, Mom. I know I promised. I'm just avoiding Dad. You know?"

"He means well, darling. Let him say sorry to you."

"I just can't have him treating me like a child and telling me who to have sex with."

"I agree. If you want to have sex with Brock, you're a grown woman. I get it."

I almost trip over in surprise. I stop walking. "Mom! I've never, ever mentioned anything about Brock and I having sex."

Mom gives me a secretive, knowing look before shrugging her shoulders. "Moms just know these things. You'll see when you're a mom one day."

"It's not about Brock... it's just in general with Dad, you know. I get Brock's his friend and all. But he still expects me to be a virgin."

"I think Dad knows it's time to admit you're not his baby girl anymore, but Brock is probably stressed over that... what do you call it - bro code? Mom chuckles softly. "Jade, men can be stupid about these things, especially when it comes to love. Susan passing so tragically wrecked him, but I know love will help heal him."

"*Love?* Mom, we can barely be in the same room without taking out each other's throats."

"Passion can be like that sometimes. Besides it's boring to always have the same opinion as each other."

I need to stop this conversation. I'm not sure which is worse right now, Dad telling me to keep away or Mom assuming I've found true love.

"Look, Mom. I'm trying to boot Charlie off my sofa right now. Can we talk later? I need to go home, make sure he's gone."

"I never did like that Charlie. Come for dinner. Your father is miserable. He misses you. He'll come around to you and Brock. You'll see."

"There is nothing to come around to, Mom."

"Okay then. But dinner is at six. Be there please, don't make me have to get your brothers involved."

"Shit no, anything but that. I'll be there." Guess that had dinner sorted, so do I really need to go to the deli? A sandwich would be nice. Plus fill in the hour I told Charlie he had in which to leave.

I'd go to dinner later. Talk to Dad. Go home to an empty place. Sounded like a reasonably uneventful night. Perfect.

***

"Mom, I'm home!" I call as I let myself in.

"In the kitchen, honey. Come through."

Dad is standing in the sitting room doorway. "What're you doing here?"

"I'm here for dinner." Okay, why is he acting like he doesn't know? So much for being miserable missing me.

I look over his shoulder and see a young, dark-haired boy on the sofa. I don't need to ask to know who he belongs to. Identical hair and profile. He gives me the biggest grin and I'm transported back to the time Brock gave me that exact smile.

"It's Kieran. Brock's son."

"I gathered that." I know who he is, but why is he here today? Is Brock coming?" I don't wait for an answer. "Anyway, I'll go see if Mom needs some help."

"I'll be in here when you're ready to apologize."

"If anyone needs to apologize, it's you," I snap back.

"Okay, you two, not in front of the child. Come on. Let's go chat. I feel like it's been ages." Mom intervenes and ushers me out to her expansive kitchen which smells amazing.

"I have a green salad and some steamed vegetables done as well. We're not quite ready yet, because we're still waiting on one person."

I stop walking. "Is Brock coming?"

"Yes, he needs a home-cooked meal."

"I'm sure his billion-dollar bank account can get him lobster." I hadn't had as much as a text message from him since he left the resort. So much for caring about my welfare.

"Jade, don't be rude. He's had a big loss. Your father had to go get him and Kieran from their Disney World vacation earlier. George Anderson had a heart attack this morning."

"What! Is he okay?"

"George is gone, dear. Brock, well, you know how he is... He seems to be coping so far. Is that Charlie gone?"

"Yeah. I wonder what I ever saw in him. He seems so different now."

"One of you grew up. I doubt Charlie ever will. I was hoping you'd see that eventually."

"Really? I thought you liked him."

"I did like him. Honey, but he isn't for you. Not enough fire in his belly."

"You never said anything."

"Because your mistakes are yours to make."

I ponder this and much more. I wander from the kitchen and I walk around the large family dining table. I miss our noisy meals, fighting and laughter around here.

"Your brothers will all be home for Christmas, so we need to make it special." My mom says, from the doorway, as if reading my mind.

"I never thought I'd say this but I miss them bossing me around a little bit."

"We all just love you, Jade, and we want to keep you safe. I never thought I'd get a girl, or any other babies for that matter. I had rounds of IVF all unsuccessful. It took its toll and eventually, I decided to be at peace with it."

"I'm sorry, Mom. I never knew you'd gone through that."

My mom smiles. "Then we had a miracle. I was pregnant with you. That's why we are all so protective. But it's time you were seen as an adult by your father and brothers."

"I probably haven't done much to assist with that perception. I do need to be open and honest with Dad."

"Maybe you need to be open and honest with yourself too. Love isn't always where you expect to find it."

"It certainly isn't with Charlie."

"What about Brock?

I feel my face redden. "Don't go there, Mom. We fight and argue more than we give each other grace. He's not interested in a relationship. Especially not with me and he's so much older than me. I mean, can that age gap even work in real life?"

"I guess anything can work if you want it." Mom finished setting the table.

A knock came to the door. "Go answer that for me, Jade. Let Brock in."

I exhaled. Guess I had to face him sometime and he'd had a bad day, so I better at least offer some support, I think we are friends...

I pull the door open and Brock is standing before me. His hair is a mess, his eyes are red and swollen and he has more than a few bloodied marks on his knuckles.

"Brock...geezus. Are you okay? Is anyone hurt?"

He grabbed the door surround for support. "Jade," his breath was ragged. "I can't...I can't stay for dinner."

"Dad! Hurry..." I can see he might lose it at any second. "Brock, it's okay. Come in and sit for a minute."

"No time", he waves an envelope. "Need to go."

Dad comes out. "Brock, damn. Come in and sit down, you're a mess."

He shook his head. "Kieran can't see me like this. I have letters, Gary. Boxes and boxes of letters. From my mother." He screwed his eyes shut, his mouth taking a hard line. "All these years he said she left me, that bastard. He kept her from me. If he wasn't already dead, I would kill him with my bare hands…"

I didn't have to know the full story to understand why Brock was in this state. "George. He did this to you? Said you mother left you?"

He nodded. "I just found her letters. I have to go see her. All these years she would have thought I'd never forgiven her for leaving…that I didn't want to know her." His fist was clenched hard around the letter.

"Man, that is messed up. What an asshole." Dad put his hand on Brock's shoulder. "You can't think clearly, let alone drive anywhere."

"I'm going. I have to. Can you have Kieran for me? I'll be back in a few days."

"I'll come with you," Dad says.

"Nonsense, Gary. You have that real estate case in court tomorrow, you can't just go." Mom is behind us now.

"Look at him Lisa, he can't go alone!"

"Jade can drive him. Can't you Jade?" Mom offers my services.

Thanks for that. But I wouldn't let him leave in this state.

"Sure. Mom, can you pack us some food to go. Brock, come to the bathroom and clean up a bit. Then say goodbye to Kieran. Don't just leave. Then we'll work out where we need to go and how we'll get there." I take control of this to give him some breathing space. Just like at work. I sorted the details to give him time to work on the big stuff.

"Thank you, Jade. I really need your cool head right now." Brock stepped inside.

"I got you. Just like you tried to do for me at the resort. You were right about Delaney, by the way. I'm sorry I never listened, and I was so pigheaded."

"I'm sorry I left you there." Brock's rasping tone had an edge of softness.

I couldn't stand to see him there looking like this. I just hugged him so hard and he melted into me. So what if my parents saw? I didn't care at all. I just cared about Brock who was hurting more than any person ever needed to.

10

CHAPTER TEN

Brock

We'd driven most of the night and now I sat looking at the house on the address the letters came from. Every single one had the same address. What if she's in there and what if she doesn't want to see me anymore? Maybe it's too late.

"You okay?" Jade asks. I can't be more thankful for anyone at this moment. She'd let me ramble my whole sordid past to her on the drive. Once I started it was like a floodgate opened. Things I just needed to say.

I felt empty now. Not relieved or satisfied. Just empty. I had nothing to offer this vibrant young woman. She deserved so much better than me and my emotional baggage. I'd never felt older, but right now, I feel like I'm beyond being able to fix myself in time to be an asset to anybody.

"I think so. I'm not sure I can do this."

"We're here now. There's no rush. Do you want to find a place to stay and get a shower and some sleep?"

"Maybe. I am in a bit of a state."

"Honestly, if you want to go for it right now, I'm sure everyone will understand if you're a bit rough looking."

"Everyone?"

"She may not live alone..." Jade has another valid point.

"Do you think she remarried? Maybe I have siblings... They'll hate me." Why wouldn't they? All the effort mother had put in and nothing back.

"Brock, you can't think they will blame you for what your father did?"

"Maybe I should have tried harder to find out more about her." I drag my hand through my hair. "I can't even remember what she looks like. I found her picture. She's a stranger to me."

"You aren't thinking clearly."

"I don't think I'll ever think clearly again. I know I never want anymore hurt in my life."

"Let's go find a hot shower, some food and organize what we know. You'll feel better and you'll be more composed. I don't think another few hours will matter." Jade placed her hand on mine. Her touch is soothing. But I know I can't be that forever person for her.

More than ever now, love had no place in my life. I have Kieran and that is enough. I'm not going to risk feeling the pain that always comes with loving someone, even with hating someone. Feelings had to be switched off again after this.

***

Brock emerges from the shower of the roadside hotel we'd checked into, towel around his hips. "Once again you are right, I feel a lot better after the hot shower."

"Not to mention smell a lot better. Lucky you had a case packed."

"Kieran and I had been at Disney World. I needed a break and I'd quit the job with George."

"Good for you. So, what's next?"

"I had planned to start my own marketing firm. Then this happened."

"It will all work out. You'll see."

"How about you?"

"I'm making rent and have a little left over. Thanks for asking. I'd still like to talk to you about marketing my business."

"We can do that."

She reaches her arms around my neck and traces her lips lightly down my jaw. "Can we do this?"

I want her more than anything right now. But can I keep my emotions at bay? "I'm not sure, Jade. I don't want to give out false signals. I'm not sure I can make any promises right now."

"No strings attached. Let me take the lead. Anger isn't the only way to let out emotions." She takes my hand and kisses my torn knuckles. Walls will do that to you.

Earlier, I had been determined not to read any letters right away. But I did. I opened one and my mother's love for me spilled off the page. I don't know why she couldn't have just come and gotten me, but I know George had a big dirty hand in it.

Jade unbuttons my shirt and kissed across my chest, kissing each nipple in turn. I closed my eyes and let the pleasure wash over me. Taking away the hurt and the pain. I let her lead me to the bed and I sit down. Jade's kisses are long, deep and slow. Passion ignites in me and though I'm hard for her, I'm in no hurry.

I sigh into her kisses. Her soft lips are gentle and sweet. She trails kisses down my neck, pushes me back to lay on the bed and continues downwards trails of fire to my belt. Unbuckling and unzipping, I lift my hips to allow her to remove my trousers and briefs. She continues her exploration with her lips and tongue.

I should stop her. I haven't allowed this since....my wife. I flinch a little as she circles the head of my cock with her tongue.

"Shhhh...relax. Let it happen," she coaxes, and I do relax.

Her fingers lightly brush over me, and her mouth begins its descent once more. Lowering and rising, my thrusts begin to match her rhythm. Hot and wet, her mouth is taking as much of me as she can, her hands cupping and squeezing me at the same time.

I try to speed it up but Jade forces me to stay slow. I'm looking down at her now, seeing her taking me into her mouth and loving it. Her eyes open and lock with mine. I can't break the connection, it's so real. I need to stop her but her eyes are watching me with love. I know it's love. I feel it in every part of me and I can't hold back. I explode into her mouth.

She takes it all, and sucks gently, extracting every last drop from me. It's more than I can bear right now. That look of love, that feeling deep inside me. I can't. It's not what I want. I need to end this now.

I stand up and pull on my briefs. "Look, Jade. Thanks, but I need to go and get this sorted out with my mother. I'm glad you drove me here, but I'll order you a car to take you home."

"It's fine. I can stay. I want to support you."

"No!" That was a little louder than I'd wanted it to be.

"I'll just use the bathroom if it's not taking up too much of your time."

"I'm sorry, Jade, I should never have let you go that far. I'm no good for you. Really."

She bursts back out of the bathroom. "Here we go again. People deciding what's good for me. Get close to feelings and you bail out. You know what? I don't need this drama in my life. You're right. I'm an idiot for believing that one day you could open your heart to me. I know that's not true now."

"I tried, Jade. There's just too much to deal with. I need to do this alone."

"Sure. I get that you have a lot. But if you let me I can help you through it all."

"Go back home, Jade. I'll be back tomorrow for my son. If you want to talk, call me."

"I don't want to talk. I'm done talking. One day I'll find someone who isn't afraid to love me. I hope your life works out fine. I really do, but please don't contact me either directly or indirectly. I need to move on."

"No problem." Those words did hurt, I had to admit. But better a little hurt now than ripping my heart out later. I call the car for her and when it arrived, she left, just like that. Now I need to go back to that house and knock on the door.

11

CHAPTER ELEVEN

J ade

Two months later

Woo! That's my fifth booking today and my next six months are filled with quality clients. Not only am I making rent, I can probably find a bigger place soon. I have savings in the bank. Hard to believe that before I went to work for Brock, my life was a mess.

He's never contacted me. I'd asked him not to, but somehow, I'd hoped he might fight a little harder for me once all his family turmoil had levelled out. Maybe I could contact him, but facing that rejection again isn't high on my to-do list.

I started dating. Strangely enough, all older men. I found my age shallow and boring. No one had gotten past the friend zone, but I had enjoyed some great times. Carrie and I went dancing every weekend and I seemed to want to sleep a lot lately. Alcohol just made me sick, so I stopped drinking.

Tonight was dinner at Mom and Dad's. Hadn't been there much lately. Mom tried to bring Brock up into conversation, but I asked her not try and encourage anything with him. We'd both decided this wasn't for us and she'd let it go. Sort of.

All I know is, he and Dad are firm friends again, so that definitely puts the nail in our coffin because he would never pick me over his best friend. I guess that's honorable. His marketing business was going strong by all accounts, but I wasn't sure what had happened with his mother. I didn't want to ask and make it appear like I care. Because I don't.

Life is great right now, why complicate things? I burst through the front door excited to tell them the news about my bookings list. "Mom, Dad! Guess what? I'm fully booked up for the next six months and I have savings."

"Guess I can ask you for a loan then?"

That voice stopped me in my tracks. Why is Brock here? Where are my parents?

"What's going on?" My head is spinning and he smells so damn good.

"I asked your parents to get you here."

"You agreed, no contact."

"I agreed to not call or text you."

"Loophole." I cross my arms. He looks good. Better somehow.

"I had a lot going on. I'm sorry I reverted to being an asshole. It came naturally." He steps towards me and I step back. "I'm only wanting to update you on what happened after you left."

"After you made me go, you mean."

"Yes, after I made you go." He sighed. "I'm truly sorry, Jade. I never wanted to hurt you and I did exactly that."

"What did happen after I left?"

He held out his hand. "Let's go into the dining room, I've arranged dinner and wine for us."

"No wine for me. Makes me ill." I place my hand in his and immediately want to rip it away again because it feels so perfect encased in his warm hand.

"No problem. Come sit, I have a lot to tell you."

He pulls the chair out for me and I sit as he pushes it in under me.

"Thank you." This food smells delicious. I can see it's not Mom's cooking.

"We have a lobster starter whenever you're ready. But first, let's talk."

"Great."

"So when I went back to the house, a man answered the door. He's my half-brother and five years younger than me. Turns out I have two sisters and a brother. They all have kids, so Kieran has cousins. It's amazing."

"Your mother?" I hardly want to ask, but I have to know.

His eyes went downward and when he looked back up tears shone on his cheeks. Real tears, from Brock! He didn't even seem bothered that I see them.

"She's passed, two years ago."

"Oh Brock, I am so, so sorry."

"So am I. But I learned so much and I know I was truly loved by her and wanted. George kept her away by saying if she tried to contact me, he'd take me somewhere she could never find me. He kept her updated with information on my progress with grades and things. He told her I didn't want to see her because she'd left. He was cheating on her constantly and she couldn't just sit by and watch."

"That man has a lot to answer for in the next life." I say and I hear the emotion in Brock's voice, He's letting the feelings happen, not covering it with anger.

"She never knew I hadn't seen any of her letters. She kept a birthday present every year for me."

I couldn't help it. I burst into tears at this. "Oh that poor woman. How she must have suffered."

"Her name was Miranda. She was broken-hearted but she fell in love and remarried. She wanted a happy life and she wanted to leave a legacy of happiness there for me, so I would always be surrounded by love if I ever found my way to them. She knew George would suck everything from me but she had high hopes that I'd rise above being like him."

"And you have. You really have. I'm so happy for you, Brock."

"Only because my mother's family; my family, welcomed me with open arms. It was the healing I finally needed. Even from losing Susan." He stood up and brought over a lobster entrée and placed it in front of me.

"Can I have some water please?" My emotions were swirling inside and the strong scent of lobster hit my nostrils. My hand flew over my mouth, and I scrambled off the chair and into the powder room. I just made it before my nausea turned to retching.

Brock is behind me, holding my hair back. "Jade, are you okay? Never known seafood to make you ill before."

I breathe in long and hard. "It's been a busy week. I think I'm just a bit off color."

"You have to take time out for rest. Your own business can run you into the ground fast if you let it." Brock helps me up. I run some water at the sink and rinse my mouth out.

"I'll get rid of the lobster. How does lamb shank and mash with gravy sound?"

"I think I can manage that."

He pulls me into his arms. "I've missed you, Jade."

I've nothing left to fight this with. "I've missed you as well."

"Do you think we can start over fresh. Without me being a total asshole?"

"I think we can start fresh, but I doubt you can stop being an asshole." I let out a giggle.

"You always did have a smart mouth." I could feel his laugh rumble from his stomach and we both started till tears poured down our faces.

"I needed that laugh. Life has been way too serious lately." I hold him closer.

"I know it's early, and there's a lot of time but I'd like to think we can get married and start a family of our own one day. Is that somewhere you can see us going?"

My heart explodes with feelings for this man showing me every vulnerability he has. But there's still one thing I need to know. "What about the bro code?"

"I've spoken to Gary. He knows how I feel about you. He was a little shocked and a little pissed. But I told him that I intended to make you my wife with or without his approval. If you'd have me. If that meant he could no longer be my friend, then so be it."

I push back and look him in the eyes. I can't believe this. "Really? What did he say?"

"We're still friends."

"This is unbelievable."

"I love you, Jade. More than life itself. I'd love for you to make me and Kieran the happiest males on earth."

"What if he doesn't like me?"

"He takes after me, so no problem there. I can't promise he won't argue with you though." He grins at me.

"I think I can handle that. Plenty of practice." Brock is everything I've ever needed in a man. I know that now. He never got friend-zoned, we were never friends. Just two people fighting against what was meant to be.

"I truly do love you..." he touches my face lightly with his fingers.

"I lo..." My hand flies back to my mouth and I'm heading for the powder room again. Oh man, way to go, Jade.

My retching starts again. Brock is chuckling behind me, my hair held back in his hands. "I guess I can say I evoked something out of you."

"I'm so sorry Brock, I don't know what's wrong with me. Maybe I ate some bad food." I retch again. "I...truly do...love...you," I say while panting and gulping for air.

"Maybe we need a pregnancy test." His words slam into my head. "What!?"

"That first night, maybe four months ago now. It's entirely possible."

"Oh dammit. No. Please. I'm not ready for that." I moan over the toilet bowl.

"We got this. If it is a baby, we'll deal with it."

Epilogue

Brock

Six months later

"Hey sexy, how's your day been?" I sidle up to Jade with her heavily swollen belly and a little extra junk in her trunk. Fuck she is so beautiful right now in the moonlight. She gets overheated so she loves to cozy up on the deckchair in the evenings.

"Sexy? I'm like a beached whale." She grins up at me. "A beached whale with swollen feet." Then bursts into tears. Fanning her face off with her hand. "Oh shit, I'm sorry, hormones get me like this." She breathes through her emotions. "I know I look like crap, but thanks for the ego boost."

"You are the most beautiful woman in the world right now." I rub her belly. "Hi Bubba, getting ready to come see Dada soon?" I bend and kiss her stomach.

"Sure, my hair is a mess. My belly is out to here. I can barely waddle to save myself."

I sink down on one knee and pull the ring box out of my pocket. I'd been talking about marriage for months but Jade insisted there was no need just because she was pregnant.

"I love you, Jade Madison. I couldn't pick a better mother for my children. Please, say yes. Will you be my wife?"

"You're asking me when I'm looking my worst?"

"Yes. Because it doesn't matter how you look. I love you for who you are and the person you make me."

I see the tears in her eyes, and I hope that means I've timed it right. Or it may mean a refusal is on the way. Her face is wet with them now. "So, does that mean yes?"

She nods. "Yes. Yes of course I will, you big lug. Now help me up off this lounge so I can kiss you."

I pull her up towards me and kiss her gently at first but she becomes more insistent. Fireworks go off and all our combined families come out from hiding.

Jade breaks out of the kiss and whacks me in the arm. "Brock! How could you plan a surprise like this when I look so awful. Also, fireworks are a bit over the top."

Kieran runs in and joins our hug. We both clutch at him. My nieces and nephews run around like they'd been coming here all their lives. My house is now a home again and more than I could ever have dreamed of.

"You look perfect. I love you. Forever."

"I love you too, darling. Forever and always."

THE END

If you liked this book then you'll LOVE my next hot romance, *Bossy Bad Boy Billionaire*!   Just click here to get yours:

https://mybook.to/rUi3

The billionaire heir with a secret is the jerk who, in college, cruelly deceived me.   Now we're fake engaged, but this time... against all odds, he's playing for keeps.

Some men are hard to forget. Like the one who hurt me by prank dating me.

Years later, I recognized Jackson with his hot-looking, chiseled features and perfectly muscled body.

He's still a jerk, only bossier.

I agreed to do all I could to clean up the presidential candidate's grandson's image – including becoming fake engaged.

It's a business arrangement right? But between annoyance and verbal sparring, a single kiss ignited sparks of mutual lust.

We agreed on a one-time tryst. Call it... closure.

But I couldn't resist the troubled grump of a man who bared both his heart and his body to me.

I've fallen for Jackson.   Again.

Jackson has a secret and the media is relentless.

He's cracking under the pressure and my world is coming undone.

This could be the end of a love I never saw coming.

My heart is aching to know- can this relationship ever be more than fake?

Get your copy here: https://geni.us/5zVMD

Turn the page to read Chapter One

Chapter One

HOPE

"Can I get you anything, Sir?" I inquire, sounding a bit too eager to my ears.

The Meridian Ball is amazing! With its expansive Palladian windows and numerous Empire chandeliers, the Astor Ballroom is one of the most historic and palatial event spaces in Washington D.C..

The band is playing and the booze is flowing. I can't believe I'm here, wearing my first ballgown and rubbing elbows with the elegantly attired, highly influential, dignitaries, political and business elite.

My palms are damp, and I hover near Mr. Rupert Bradley, the man who could very well be the next U.S. President with me as the Social Media Strategist on his campaign.

Mr. Bradley glances over his glasses at me. "I'm sorry, do I know you?" he asks, sounding dismissive.

I laugh a little too much. He's never made a joke before, so I want to be sure he thinks that I think he's funny.

"I don't have time to flirt. Could you find another man to gold dig on?" His eyes aren't smiling with good humor the way they usually are.

He's not joking. How typical. If I look glam, I must be some kind of gold digger and when I dress casually, I offend the world because I don't look like a woman should.

His eyes show no recognition. I really am slightly stunned. I've been working with him daily for the last week. Surely, I don't look *that* different.

With a gown that tastefully shows off my ample girls and hour-glass figure, Gia, my best friend, did say I'd have all the male heads turning. I scoffed at the time and said *as if*. I'm not here for male attention.

Had it once and I can live without it. I'm here to be the best and move up from social media strategist to my dream job as Campaign Manager.

"Ah, Mr. Bradley, It's me... Hope Kelly."

He takes his glasses off and appraises me up and down. "I'll be damned. Hope! Wow. Absolutely stunning."

A waiter passes by, and he grabs a glass of Champagne off the tray and hands it to me. "I have to say, I didn't think you could step in at the last second when Richard got ill. But you sure have. Here. Drink this. Try to relax."

I release my grip on my purse and take the glass and my face warms at his compliment.

I'm very nervous to be stepping in tonight but this is the sort of thing I need to get used to if I want that top job from Richard, the current Campaign Manager- and I *very* much want that job.

This is the chance I've been waiting for. Feels like I've been in school forever. Socializing has always taken a back seat. Now I'm thirty and being out and about socially still takes some getting used to.

I fish for something to say. I settle on: "Thank you for the invite,"

Mr. Bradley waves his hand as if to shoo me off like an errant schoolgirl. "You go out there and mingle a little and see if you can overhear anything that might help me win this campaign." He winks at me. "You'll be seated with my grandson and me at the dinner table —if he bothers to stop being rebellious and turn up, that is. See you then."

I take a long sip. His grandson? I hope he doesn't mean Jackson Bradley. Surely not. Jackson is barely in D.C. anymore, according to my tracking of him in the socials.

Not that I'm interested in what he's been doing since he humiliated me at college...it's part of my job to keep my finger on the pulse of anything that may blow up, and Jackson and his string of slim, blond beauties and rogue antics need constant attention.

I'm not his type. He never has curvy brunettes on his arm and I know that from experience. I was stupid to ever believe he really liked me...but his kisses, my first kisses, fooled me. His kisses...

My pulse races. Of course, it isn't him. But what if it is? Shit...what if it is him? I haven't had real Champagne for two years, but if Jackson is here and I have to sit with him, I'm gonna need a mega-hit of bravado.

Suddenly, it's grown very stuffy in here. Perhaps I'll go look at the gardens. I'm sure to spot someone I know soon, and a familiar face will help me relax and feel less like an imposter.

Outside, I wander along the roses, so beautiful under the lighting. I look at how they've weaved tiny lights through all the trees, like fairyland. But, there's still a good amount of light necessary for people watching. Every person here is either rich or important, or both. I'm neither... yet.

"Hey. I don't know you. You look lonely." A male voice speaks from behind me.

I turn and a round-face man with thinning hair in a comb-over, wearing a tuxedo jacket with protesting buttons, is suddenly in my personal space. A sour whiff of rum hits my nostrils.

I dodge sideways to the corner of the pergola. He follows.

"Don't run away. We can get to know each other better. I'm Harry."

"Harry, nice to meet you. I'm waiting for my boyfriend to get me a drink. So, if you don't mind, I'd prefer to wait alone." I ignore his eyes that appear to be busy undressing me, and I can't think of anything else to say.

"You're lying. I can tell." He presses his pudgy body even closer to me.

"I do prefer to be alone. So please back up." My voice is not as commanding as I hoped.

"Oh, come on. You women only dress like this for male attention, so don't play hard to get."

He touches my upper arm and disgust races through me. "Don't touch me," I snap.

"Sure." His hand runs the length of my arm now and I roughly pull it back.

I'm about to knee him in the groin for real. In high school and college, I used to be the brunt of taunts and pranks. I learned the hard way how to handle myself.

If I knee him, it will draw attention, but putting a positive spin to that on social media wouldn't be so hard. It's what I'm best at and what got me this job opportunity.

I put temptation aside because I don't know who he is, and damaging the nuts of someone important could get me off this campaign. No matter how much he deserves it, I've worked too hard to ruin it now.

"Harry, stop being an asshole." A deep voice I remember too well sounds from behind us. My heart starts pounding. I don't look behind Harry to acknowledge the newcomer.

It's Jackson, I know it, the last person I wanted to see tonight, or ever.

Harry's face changes from fake-friendly to hatred but he doesn't move away from me. "What business is it of yours, *cousin*?"

Cousin? Is this Harry related to Mr. Bradley as well? I risk a glance behind Harry. Geezus, Jackson is impossibly broader, taller and more attractive than I remember.

He glances at me before returning his hard stare to Harry.

"You know I don't care about being arrested again for hitting you, don't you?" Jackson grins wolfishly.

Harry licks his lips and backs away a step. "Won't look good for the campaign."

"Worth it." Jackson grips Harry's shoulder and pulls him further away from me.

"Fine. She's a frigid bitch, anyway. Good luck." Harry shrugs off Jackson's grip and storms back inside.

I look up and I see a wavy mop-top of dark blond hair, steel blue eyes and an unshaven face. None of that detract from the fine form he cuts in his tuxedo.

Damn, Jackson looks good. Can my night get worse? How I hated this man in college for what he'd done to me. He is my best times and worst time at college all rolled into one.

Him and his popular group—all gorgeous and perfect, but assholes to anyone who wasn't to their liking. Like me.

Show off your curves. Be proud of what your momma gave you. That's what the magazines said, but all I got for trying to wear fashionable clothes was laughed at for not being a size 0.

Jackson fake-dated me for a dare—which I could have lived with if he hadn't persuaded me into exchanging kisses with him that felt so real.

It's been years but the memories bring back of a flood of my old insecurities. Aren't I over this crap already?

"I'm Jackson Bradley." His eyes study mine as he holds his fist out for a bump.

I look away. Clearly, he has no clue who I am, and it's probably better to keep it that way. "I was about to knee Harry in the balls. But thanks."

"*That*, I'd love to have seen." He drops his fist, unbumped. "Harry's a distant cousin on my mother's side... don't hold that against me. What an ass."

I so want to say, 'it runs in the family,' but I bite my tongue. "Making a public scene in the middle of campaign season made me hesitate. Plus, I didn't know who he was. I didn't want to crush the nuts of some important foreign diplomat," I say instead.

"Ugh. Another solid reason to hate the campaign. Ruins all my fun." He looks distant for a second before turning his bright eyes on me, "Anyway, want a drink? Your glass is empty."

Why is my heart still galloping? I don't want to make small talk with the man who made me fall for him and then laughed with his friends as he took the bet money for fake dating me. Shit happens. No doubt we've both changed a lot, but I still have no desire to go back to feeling like the insecure girl I used to be.

I guess it was wishful thinking to support and work for his grandfather and think I'd never run into him. Especially when I'm Social Media Manager and Jackson is blowing up the social media platforms every other day.

"I'm good." I walk past him, and I feel his eyes watching as I move away.

Damn these natural curves. I can't tame the sway in this dress and heels. I need my black jeans, oversized shirt and flat boots back.

I see the bathroom sign. Thank goodness. I grab another champagne off a tray and drink half.

Eight years since I'd seen Jackson Bradley. I was never in any hurry to see him again. Yes, he is major eye candy, but devastatingly good looks can't account for a mean heart.

He made it clear how he feels about curvy women and about me.

Clearly, I had no effect on him. He doesn't even remember me.

I place my drink on a side table and go into the bathroom.

I check myself quickly in the mirror, no panda-eyes from mascara, long dark curls in place, and the red lipstick still looks good. It's hard for me to believe it's me.

A few other women are doing the same and chattering.

"Did you see his Ferrari?" One of the super-slim ladies wearing a gold dress and dripping diamond jewelry says. She looks like she's off the cover of a glossy magazine.

Although I look great, and very different for me, I'm don't feel in the league of these cultured women.

"I know. What I wouldn't give for thirty minutes with Jackson Bradley. He can throw me around anytime!" Another said, and they both giggled.

"I hear he's an animal in the bedroom."

My eyes roll automatically as I head out of the bathroom.

My text message alert sounds from inside the emerald green purse that I was so excited to match with my shimmering ball gown. I scramble to get it out and almost drop it before I see the text.

It's Mr. Bradley. Oh no.

Where are you?

Bathroom, sorry, I message back,

Meet where we were before. Hurry

Ok

What's going on? This seems weird. I see Mr. Bradley standing across the expansive ballroom and head towards him.

I can see his expression the closer I get and his frown doesn't give me confidence. I hope it isn't me he's mad at. Maybe he heard about the incident outside with Harry.

I get to him as fast as I can in these unfamiliar block heels.

"Hope. Do you mind skipping dinner?" he asks.

My stomach murmurs a little. "That's fine, what's up?"

I realize from previous jobs with political candidates that sleeping, eating and even bathing sometimes take a backseat.

"My boneheaded grandson is what's up. He's out there chatting up the Sheik's niece, and if I don't get him away from her, we may have diplomatic problems."

"What can I do?" I'm immediately in full-on damage control mode.

"I'm running a 'family-values', an 'all-people-deserve-a-decent-standard-of-living' campaign. He needs to stop flaunting our wealth and get a job. My campaign can't afford any more of his shenanigans. Twice last month I had to bail him out for speeding and being a public nuisance. He needs to grow the fuck up." Mr. Bradley's voice descends to a low growl.

"I don't care how you do it, Hope, just get him out of here and get him looking good online."

Wait, what? Great, now I have to perform the impossible with the last person on the planet I needed to spend time with.

I quickly follow his long strides heading outside. We dodge our way through an obstacle course of wait staff and well-heeled guests.

We're outside again now and I see a beautifully exotic young woman as thin as a reed wearing colorful silks.

Get your copy on Amazon here: https://mybook.to/rUi3

About the Author

Aria McDow is an author bringing contemporary romances to readers who love stories featuring hot as-all-get-out men who have just that right mix of power, charisma, and hidden vulnerability, and sassy, smart women who turn their worlds upside down. Aria is an angst junkie who believes in true love. Whether a billionaire, professor, or grumpy boss, every book is guaranteed a happy ending and readers will enjoy a rich, bumpy ride to get there. Aria lives in Virginia and started her own love affair with romance books when she read them clandestinely in middle school.

She enjoys travel, drawing and hanging upside from rollercoasters. The best part of life is being retired from the military and having time to create as well as enjoy her family, especially her new grandbaby.

Want to be the first to learn about Aria McDow's new releases? Click the link and "Follow" her on the top left corner of the Amazon page.

https://www.amazon.com/stores/Aria-McDow/author/B0C95F1Z59

Want to read Aria McDow's next releases for FREE? Sign up for her Newsletter and from there, Join her ARC Team here and read and review all her upcoming releases for FREE: https://dl.bookfunnel.com/31y4jk1yep